A FATHER'S
FIGHT

A FATHER'S
FIGHT

Blake and Layla #2

JB SALSBURY

A Father's Fight
J.B. Salsbury

Copyright © 2015 J.B. Salsbury

ISBN: 1507547625
ISBN-13: 9781507547625

Edited by Theresa Wegand

Cover by Amanda Simpson of Pixel Mischief Design

To my Fighting Girls

Fight on, and if you must go down, go down swinging.

PROLOGUE

Eighteen years ago...

I can't believe I'm going to do this. This isn't my first high school party, but damn, it might as well be.

I suck back a lungful of crisp evening air that swirls with the stench of cigarettes and pot then try to shake feeling back into my hands. It's cold, or maybe it's my nerves, but either way, I can't feel my fingers.

"Come on," I whisper-yell to myself. "Don't be such a wuss!"

Giggles filter to me from a group of passing girls. With a hip to my '78 Trans-Am, I stare boldly at the cluster of hot pink and skin as they scoff and point at my ride. It may not be the first choice of most sixteen-year-olds, but it's been my dream car since seventh grade. Those chicks can have their Mustangs and their Jettas. My car has a personality and an attitude.

"White trash," the head fluff-bunny says through a cough.

These girls couldn't be more opposite of me. They're the bright to my plain, the color to my black, the Spice Girls to my Metallica. Dressed in the same color pattern as a candy shop, with big billowing curls, bright lips, and about half the amount of clothes on that I do, they don't seem the least bit cold.

I glare at their retreating asses, hardly covered by their school-girl-stripper skirts. I guess now's as good a time as any. No more stalling.

I head to the open gate that leads into the backyard of a middle-class home in the Seattle 'burbs. Pushing through a crowd of teenagers that huddle around the entrance, I search for a familiar face and find nothing but drones. Carbon copies of whatever's hot on MTV. Zero individuality, every single one of them, except one. The only person I came here to see. My stomach flips on itself, and I run my sweaty—yet cold—palms along my skinny jeans.

I'm finally going to approach my crush, the guy I've been loving from afar since the first day of freshman year.

Trip Miller.

While casually stalking him last week, I overheard him mention this party to his friends. I contemplated coming for all of zero seconds. This is what I've been waiting for, the chance I've needed. If he shows up, I'll be here waiting, and for the first time, I refuse to let my nerves get the better of me.

I'm going to talk to him.

A flutter of excitement tumbles in my chest. My fingers go numb again, and I straighten my cut-up Whitesnake tee that I'd shredded in the back to show off my blue bra. It's not the thigh-high socks and mini-skirts that all the other girls are wearing, but I refuse to conform.

My toe taps inside my monkey boot as I wait in line to get in, and my fingers sift through and twirl the ends of my hair. The weather this time of year isn't as humid, and I've managed to flat iron my hair so it hangs in sleek panels down past my boobs.

"Five bucks, midget," a big guy manning the door wearing a letterman jacket barks down at me, taking me in with a scowl.

How original. I dip my chin to roll my eyes without him seeing and pull a wadded up five-dollar bill from my back pocket. He's a senior and a football player, according to his jacket. He's big, with a shaved head, and looks like all the other popular guys, a member of the crew that earns friends by intimidation and bullying those who are weaker.

He stamps my hand and shoves a red Solo cup at me.

"Thanks." I move into the backyard and toward the sound of Snoop Dogg's "Murder was the Case." I bet the rapper would lock himself in the Dog Pound if he knew how many jocks were dressing like him and adding "izzles" to almost every word they spoke.

I head on back to a couple staggered lines that lead to kegs and take my place in one of them. I'll grab a beer, mingle a bit. There are enough kids here from other schools that it shouldn't be too hard to fall into a conversation with someone. Then I can sit back and watch, waiting for the one guy who's ever gotten my heart to thunder in my chest.

As if the thought of him alone triggered my inner stalker, I scan the crowd, searching. A bright smile catches my eye, not so much because it's attractive but because it's so blatantly obvious. I know that guy; he's in one my classes. *Why is he smiling at me?* Maybe it's someone else he's scoping. I turn to glance over my shoulder. Nope, it's me.

I toss him what I'm sure is an awkward smile-wave combo. He tilts his head, and his expression goes soft. Dammit, maybe that was a mistake. I should wait in my car. I could spy from the street until—Oh God, he's coming this way.

Kids scurry to clear a path as he struts toward me. He's as big as the others and hot shit on campus. His striking blond hair is spiked, and his clean-shaven face and cologne scream of a man who spent more time getting ready for tonight than I did.

"Hey." He starts talking with still a few feet between us. "Layla…right?" And now he's right up in my space.

I rock back to try to gain a few inches between us. "Yeah, um…" I squint one eye. "I'm sorry, but I don't remember your name."

He smiles in way that feels patronizing, as if it's absurd that I wouldn't know who he is. "Stewart."

I snap my fingers. "That's right." I don't really remember, but it does sound a little familiar now. I think.

"Wow, you look"—he drops his gaze to my feet then makes his way back up to my eyes—"really interesting."

"Thanks?"—I shake my head and desperately need something to do with my hands, so I fumble with my cup—"I think."

Where do we go after the non-compliment? My cheeks flame as his gaze burns against my skin. An awkward silence builds between us, and it's almost as if he's finding enjoyment in watching me squirm.

"It's um…colder than I thought it'd be." It's lame, but I'm desperate for a diversion, something that will get his eyes off me.

He blinks, jerked from whatever he was thinking about. "Oh yeah, you cold?" He starts to shrug off his letterman jacket.

"No!" I hold up my hand.

He freezes and his eyes narrow.

I clear my throat. "I'm sorry. I mean no thanks. I'm good. I think I just need a beer. That'll help." A stupid girlie laugh falls from my lips, and I internally growl at how easily this guy can unnerve me.

"Suit yourself." He adjusts the collar of his jacket and slides his gaze down the line of people waiting for the keg, me being at the end of the line. "You're going to be waiting here all night."

The line moves up one tiny step, punctuating his statement.

More silence.

"Yeah, well…" Well what? *This is freakin' painful.* Maybe if I turn my back on him, he'll leave.

"How 'bout this?" He moves in closer to me, leaning to say something in my ear. "See that?" He nods toward a fire pit, his hot breath blowing against my skin.

"Yeah?" I swallow hard, nervous about how close he is. Why has this guy never made an effort to talk to me before, and now he won't freakin' leave me alone? Or give me room to breathe?

"Why don't you come over there with me? We've got a small ice chest with some beers, shots, and mixed drinks." He leans back, his blue eyes flashing with…what is it? Humor? Excitement?

I avoid whatever it is and turn back toward the crowd clustered around the fire. The heat of the flames is enticing, but the company is absolutely not. It's them, the popular kids: a group of guys in various forms of preppy flannel shirts and khakis, and girls in half-shirts more appropriate for a weekend in Florida than Seattle.

"That's okay, but thanks." I motion to the line with my empty cup. "I'll take my chances here."

He tilts his head again, giving me a look as if he's trying to read my soul but then flashes a smile that's friendly and even kind. "We don't bite, Layla."

"Ha!" *That's it? Ha!*

"Come on. You're practically shivering." His logic can't be argued. I am shivering, although it has little to do with the temperature. "At least come grab a beer with us and warm up until the line dies down." He lifts one eyebrow.

Pushing up on tiptoes, I lean around the people in front of me to see how much further I have to go. The sound of cheering comes from the keg. What the—?

"Keg stands." He shrugs one shoulder and takes a sip of his beer. "They'll probably go on most of the night."

I worry my lip with my teeth. Crap! I was hoping for a tiny bit of liquid courage before I faced Trip. The fire does look nice. Maybe one beer and a warm up? Surely I can avoid conversation for one beer, not that any of them will want to talk to me. And from that side of the yard, I'd have a better vantage point for seeking out Trip.

"Okay, sure." I throw my shoulders back and nod. "One beer."

His face lights up in a wide smile, teeth too white and a little too straight. Are they fake? "Great." He grabs my hand— grabs my fucking *hand*—and leads me to his friends.

Flashes of every teen-nerd movie I've ever seen flicker through my mind. I'll end up the butt of one of their pranks, something I've seen many times over the last two years of high school, the very reason I keep my head down around them.

I tug my hand, ready to make the excuse that I have to run out to my car and get something. I see a hint of black leather and a gasp falls from my lips.

He's here. My heart kicks double-time, breath speeds up, and goose bumps skate down my arms.

Trip.

He's leaning against the wall, red cup in hand with a cigarette pinched between two fingers. He's nothing like the other guys in school, and even the other rocker dudes he hangs with have more of a grungy, in-need-of-a-shower, Kurt Cobain thing going on. But not Trip.

Shaggy hair the color of milk chocolate hangs down over his ears and what I know to be icy-blue eyes. I dig his style: black jeans, Doc Martens, and a black concert tee that I can't quite make out under his leather biker jacket, complete with zippers and buckles.

Has God ever made a more beautiful boy?

The spice of his cologne mixed with cigarette smoke and the buttery scent of leather gets me every time I pass by him in school. And even now, even though I can't smell him, my stomach dips at the thought.

He must feel my ogling because, as I'm being dragged across the yard, his eyes meet mine. I suck in a quick breath and stare in fascination as he narrows his glare and takes a long drag off his cigarette. As the cherry on the end glows bright orange, the heat in my body expands.

"What the hell are you doin', Stewart?" A female voice sounds pissed off and I'm jerked to a halt.

I'm forced to rip my eyes away from Trip and realize I'm a foot away from the fire and engulfed in the popular crowd.

"Chill out, Daphne," Stewart says, sounding bored, bends over, and reaches into a large ice chest, still keeping hold of my hand.

It's the girl from out front. I try to wriggle my hand free, but he only holds it tighter. Maybe because this Daphne girl is giving me the evil eye he's keeping me close?

She rolls her over-made-up eyes as if Stewart brought home a stupid toy to play with. "What's up with the goth chick?"

I hate dumb girls. "I'm not goth." Not that it matters. I'm actually kind of hoping they kick me out so I can go talk to Trip who…I slide my gaze over to him, and he's now leaning with his shoulder against the wall, his back toward me. Dammit.

"Goth, Hessian, whatever." She crosses her arms over her chest and kicks out a hip. "Go hang with your people. You're not wanted here."

"Easy, Daph." Stewart stands in front of me, and I finally pull free my hand. "She's with me."

I cringe. "No, I'm no—"

"Stew," Daphne says in that overly affected whiney way girls do when they're trying to get what they want.

"Leave it alone." Stewart's words carry a threat, but he turns his back on her, and his bright eyes and smile are fixed on me with kindness.

She huffs out a breath but turns without another complaint and stalks away.

"Sorry about that." His eyes are intense, and his expression is genuinely apologetic. "Here." He hands me a water bottle filled with red juice. "Peace offering."

I grab it, give it a quick onceover, but can't help my eyes from searching out Trip. "What is it?"

"Jungle juice." He throws an arm over my shoulder and guides me to a seat close to the fire. "Two parts fruit punch, two parts vodka, and a healthy shot of lime juice."

The urgency to find Trip rides me hard. If I don't talk to him before he leaves, this entire night is nothing but a fat waste of time. I unscrew the lid, give it a sniff, and recoil slightly.

Stewart laughs. "Oh come on. It doesn't smell that bad." He lifts one eyebrow. "Does it?"

A grin pulls at my lips. This guy is kind of funny. "No, it's fruity, but…" I take a sip and shiver as the liquid fire rolls down my throat. "Whoa."

"It's strong. Just have a couple shots. You'll warm up in no time." He winks and takes a long pull off his beer.

I take another swig of jungle juice, hoping to hide behind the bottle. I dart my gaze over to Trip, who is talking but stops for a split second to study me, his eyes moving between me and Stewart.

Freshman and sophomore year Trip didn't know I existed, but so far, even only a month into our junior year, I've caught him watching me. Never for more than a second, and he's never attempted to talk to me, but there's something there.

Right?

Just as quickly as the thought runs through my head, he turns his back on me. I came here on a singular mission. I will brave a conversation with Trip before this night is over.

I smile and take another swig, contemplating my plan of action. I just need to confront him, introduce myself, and see where the conversation leads. I take another long pull from the juice. Huh…it actually doesn't taste too bad.

"You warming up?" Stewart nods to the water bottle I have pressed to my lips.

"Hmm? Mm-hm." I choke back another shot-worth.

He watches me swallow and lick the sweet sticky stuff off my lips. "That's good, Laylay."

I cringe at his ridiculous nickname. *He doesn't even know me!*

"Here." He cracks the pop-top and hands me an ice cold can of beer he must've pulled from the ice chest. "Chaser."

"Thanks." My tongue is suddenly ten times bigger than it was when I got here. But, damn…I feel great: strong, ballsy, and ready to break through any weird tension that lingers between me and Trip.

"Cheers." Stewart holds up his cup. "To a life-altering night."

Fuck yeah! "Absolutely!"

A tap of our drinks moves in slow motion. Whoa…I blink and try to hold open my heavy eyes. Eh…screw it. I let them droop, feeling too good to fight it.

Another sip, then another, and…

ONE

Present Day

BLAKE

It never fails.

Sprawled on my patio lounger, legs crossed at the ankles, the tip of my nose feels numb against the mid-January early morning chill. I pull my beanie down low over my ears with one hand, while my finger absently toys with the corner of a printed and folded up email I have shoved in my jeans pocket. The flimsy paper curls beneath my thumb, worn thin from carrying it around and reading it with the hope that something will pop out at me: a clue as to what it all means. If nothing else, carrying it is a good reminder of what I have to deal with and soon.

Go figure. When life finally starts smelling like roses, there's always something that comes along to drop a big fat fucking shit on my damn bouquet. If I could put myself in a headlock, choke myself out for being such a pussy, I would, but unless I miraculously become a double-jointed contortionist, I need to face this head on.

But how?

An uneasy flutter batters the backside of my ribs, and I don't have to wonder what's bringing on the distress. I remember it all too well.

Fear.

The last time I was scared, before I met Layla, was the night I was dragged from my fuckin' bed by dudes in masks and taken to military school. Nothing since then has truly terrified me, not the toughest drill sergeants in boot camp or the possibility of going to war. Hell, not even my first MMA fight scared me. I craved battle, fucking thirsted for it.

But this is one fight I'm afraid to face because it involves the people I love most in the entire world.

Ever since Stew went to jail, Layla, Axelle, and I have been trying to build a life together. It's been the best nine months of my life, watching my woman's body change as she goes through the various stages of pregnancy, but it hasn't all been a fucking party.

Axelle's been struggling with the knowledge that her biological father is a rapist. Layla's dealing with guilt. It's two steps forward and three steps back some days, and the idea that someone could breeze on in and cause them to relive any of the shit they're finally getting through fires my blood.

I blow out a shaky breath. *Calm down. Don't lose your shit.* The email is not a threat, at least, not yet. My hands ball into fists, gripping the inside of my jeans pockets, one crushing the email, as I watch the sun peek up over the distant hills.

The sound of the sliding glass door yanks me from my thoughts, and I jump from the lounger and whirl around. "Mouse, baby…no." I move to block Layla before she's able to step one socked foot outside. "It's too cold. You need—"

"Blake." Her big brown eyes are pulled tight.

Fuck, it's that tone—the tone that precedes the tongue-lashing that never fails to make my lips curl and my dick jump—but she's crazy if she thinks turning me on is going to make me change my mind.

"I'm pregnant, not sick. I'm fully capable of being outside." Her voice carries the rough edge of morning, and her eyes are a little puffy from sleep.

She's never looked so beautiful.

I open my mouth to argue and even move to usher her inside, but her glare stops both.

"Look." She motions to her body, which is still so fuckin' tiny except for her round belly. "Sweatshirt, leggings." She lifts a foot and wobbles, but I grab her to keep her steady. "Thick socks. I'm bundled."

"I know, but it's cold and flu season, and I don't think we should take any chances." I rub her arms and hope to push her deeper into the house, but she doesn't budge. "Fuck, you're stubborn as hell."

She lifts an eyebrow. "Blake, we live in Las Vegas. It's gotta be sixty degrees outside."

I shrug and check my phone. "Fifty-two."

"Let me out. I'll even do this." She pulls the hoodie of her sweatshirt over her head and tugs the drawstrings so tight that the only part of her face that shows is her nose and her lips. "There. Happy?"

I bite my lip to avoid the laugh that's forcing its way up my throat. "Not yet." I scoop her up into my arms, and she squeals, having not seen it coming. Her warm little body, ripe with my growing baby, does weird shit to my chest. Having nine months to figure out what that is, I've come to identify it as a mix of arousal and worship, and I don't know what to do first, make love to her or make a damn sacrifice in her honor.

In seconds, I have her to the lounger where I drop down and arrange her comfortably between my legs. Her left hand rests for a moment on my thigh, and I catch the glint of her engagement ring. My lungs release a tiny bit of the air I didn't know I was hanging on to.

The solitaire black diamond I put on her finger on New Year's Eve after making love to her in our bed is a meaningful reminder that she's mine.

She loosens the drawstrings on her sweatshirt to reveal her entire face and then nuzzles into my chest. "Mmm… yeah, I like this better."

"Yeah, me too." I flex my hips, showing her how happy her proximity makes me. This woman never fails to arouse me just by pressing close.

A tiny giggle bubbles from her lips. "I can tell." Her arms wrap tighter around my middle, and with one hand on her belly, I rub circles on her back. "You wanna talk about it?"

My hand freezes for a split second before I get my shit in check and act nonchalantly. "Always like talkin' about my dick, Mouse. You start."

Her low chuckle vibrates against my chest. "Not that." She tilts her head back so her coffee-colored eyes meet mine. "About why you're not sleeping."

Unable to look her in the eye, I swing my gaze back toward the upcoming sun. "Not tired. Been going to bed with you every night, so I wake up earlier."

I can feel her eyes on me but force myself to not look. "Bullshit."

My eyes jerk to hers.

"You don't think I notice when you get out of bed in the middle of the night? Or that I don't hear you in your music room?" She drops her cheek back to my chest. "I get up every fifteen minutes to pee, Blake. You're not sleeping."

A groan grinds its way up my throat. I can't tell her the shit that's been running through my head on a loop or about the damn email that's been fucking with my head. The most important things she needs from me are my love and my protection. She's walking around with a life one hundred percent dependent on her, and she needs to know she's safe. The last thing she wants to hear is that the man who's in charge of protecting her is a scared little bitch.

"I'm good." I drop a kiss on the top of her head and hope she doesn't see through my lie. "Just busy at the gym."

Weakest excuse ever.

"Right." Yep, she's not buying it. Shocker. She'd be more likely to believe I'm grumpy after being abducted and anally probed by aliens.

Time for a subject change. "What's on your agenda today?"

She takes a big breath, almost as if she's sighing in defeat. "I have to go back to the doctor today."

"What?" My body tenses. "Why?"

Her hand runs up the back of my sweatshirt and around to my bare chest and I swallow the moan that her touch always brings. "Don't worry. It's routine this far along in pregnancy. They're just checking to see if I'm dilated, effaced, and if I've lost my mucus plug, which…"

Mucus. What the fuck?

"…pretty sure I'd know if I had what looks like a dead, bloody, jellyfish drop out of my crotch."

"Whoa. Just…no. I love your pussy, Mouse. Not sure I can handle the thought of…" I shiver. "Ugh."

She pushes up, a huge smile lighting her face. "Well, well, well…The Snake isn't so tough after all, huh?"

"Mucus plug?" I cringe and swallow back saliva that pools in my throat.

"If you have a problem with *that*, then childbirth is going to be difficult for you."

"Nah…I'm good." *Fuck, I'm so not good.* "I won't let you down, Mouse. You know that, right?" *Even if it kills me.*

She drops back to my chest, and her arms encircle my middle. "I know. Just—" Her body jolts, and she pulls her vibrating cell from the pocket of her sweatshirt. She stares, silences it, and then shoves it back into her pocket. "Anyway, this is a lot more than most people should have to handle in a year. You went from living the life of a man whore—"

I smack her sweet ass.

She giggles and sinks in deeper between my legs. "A bachelor."

"Thank you."

"Now you've got a live-in girlfriend—"

"Future wife."

"—with a teenage daughter and a baby on the way. That's a lot."

I pull her chin up so I can meet her eyes. "There any doubt in your mind that I don't want—wouldn't beg—for what I have now?"

"No."

"Good girl." I drop a kiss onto her forehead and search for a change of subject. "Who just called? It's not even seven a.m."

She shakes her head. "Don't know. Unavailable. Probably a telemarketer." Her voice is tense somehow, but whether that's from the phone call or our conversation, I'm not sure. "Blake, just promise me if this becomes, I don't know, too much, you'll talk to me."

"Yeah, babe, I'll do that." *I'm a lying sack of crap.*

Her tiny body is on her side and between my legs, hands on my back, and cheek to my chest, and I'd do anything for this woman. Fuckin' anything.

Except that.

TWO

LAYLA

"You didn't have to come with me." I rock side to side on my butt to scoot back on the table, the crinkling sound of my paper gown bouncing off the walls of the exam room. As every day brings me closer to my due date, it's getting harder and harder to move.

Blake glares at me from his position on the wall, leaning, arms crossed, and looking more uncomfortable than I've ever seen him. "Why wouldn't I come with you?"

I study him, head to toe, and even though he's nervous, his presence alone fills the room. A tiny grin pulls at my lips. "Um…maybe because you look about as comfortable as a nun in a sex-toy shop."

"I've been to a couple of your appointments before." His Adam's apple bobs, and I can make out the pinch of his eyebrows beneath the low brim of his black ball cap.

"You came to the first and my ultrasound. This time I'll get a *physical* exam." My eyes widen and dart to the stirrups, trying to communicate what I'm saying without actually having to say it.

He cringes slightly and drops his gaze to his feet. *Message received.*

With his chin to his chest and his eyes off me, I use this moment to admire him fully. Big arms are encased in a red long-sleeved T-shirt, which hugs every rigid muscle I've explored, memorized, over the last ten months. Jeans hang low on narrow hips but pull tighter at his thighs. My tongue darts out to moisten my lips, and I'm lost to my thoughts of Blake naked. Raging pregnancy hormones have turned me into some sort of sexual maniac.

"Mouse." The way he drags out my nickname on a growl draws my eyes to his piercing green ones below the brim of his hat. "You're already naked, with nothing between us but some flimsy-ass paper gown. I'm not above stepping between your legs right here if you keep lookin' at me like that."

I clear what I'm sure will be a lusty rasp to my voice with a close-mouthed cough. "Oh, sorry, and no, let's not traumatize the staff." My actions contradict my words as my eyes continue to study his thick neck, shoulders, chest—

"Fuckin' hell, woman." He moves but freezes when a soft knock sounds at the door.

My eyes dart to his, and I stifle a giggle at the look of disappointment that washes over Blake's face. "Come in!"

The door opens, and in walks a nurse I've seen on a few of my previous visits. "Hey, Layla." She startles slightly when she catches Blake, who has resumed his position at the wall. "Oh hey." With a hand extended, she shakes Blake's. "Nice to see you again. I'm Cassie, Dr. Evan's assistant."

"Yeah, I remember. Blake." He nods and leans back against the wall.

Cassie's eyes come to mine. She's young. If I had to guess, I'd say she's around Blake's age, with a round face, big eyes, and the kind of skin that's probably never seen an ounce of makeup, not that she needs it.

She flashes me a kind smile. "So, Layla, are you getting excited? This could happen any day now."

Butterflies explode in my belly, or is that the baby, heartburn? "I'm excited, yeah, but also a little sick of feeling like a stuffed turkey."

"You're ready, which is totally understandable at thirty-eight weeks." She pulls up a rolling stool and opens her file folder to ask me some routine questions. "Any sign of the mucus plug?"

Blake groans until he notices us staring at him. "My bad. Go on."

What a baby! And even still my stomach does somersaults at his childlike sensitivity to all things mucus.

A few more questions and Cassie stands. "Okay, everything looks good. I'll let Dr. Cole know that you're ready. We'll check to see if you're dilated and/or effaced, and send you on your way."

"Great. Thanks, Cassie." She exits the room, and I search out Blake, who has now taken a nearby chair and looks a little pale. "Blake, you okay?"

He leans back, pulls his hat off to run a hand through his cropped hair, and then pops his hat back on. "Yeah, I'm good. It's just…" His gaze sweeps over my bare belly, which is poking out from the open front of my gown. "I know it's stupid. I just hate anyone seeing you naked, touching you…down there…" He shakes his head. "Fuck, sounds ridiculous hearing me say it."

Warmth spreads through my chest. "I kinda like that you want my nakedness to be for your eyes alone. But it's the OB and it's important."

"I know. I'm sorry. It's just…" He tilts his head to peer up at me. "Will it hurt?"

"No, it doesn't hurt. They just check my cervix with their fingers and—"

"That's enough." He holds up his hand. "I don't want to know."

I giggle. "It's no different from when you use your fingers—"

"Oh hell no." His head swivels from side to side. "It better be different. It better be a fuckuvalot different, Mouse." He rubs his eyes. "Great, now I've got that visual runnin' through my head."

"I love you, Blake Daniels." I outstretch my arm. "Now get over here and hold my hand."

He pushes to standing and takes my hand, bringing my knuckles to his lips just before another small knock sounds at the door.

"Come in," Blake says, his eyes locked on mine.

The door swings open. "Sorry to keep you waiting."

I can't see the doctor with Blake's big body obstructing my view, but what I can see is Blake's eyes, the green barely visible behind his tightly slit lids. In unison we slide our gazes off each other and toward the OB who is standing just inside the room next to Cassie.

It's not my usual doctor, which I expected because they told me Dr. Evans was on call and delivering a baby. No, this doctor is not her. He's a *he*. And a handsome he at that.

He smiles, his teeth straight and white. "Ms. Moorehead, I'm—"

"Daniels." Blake's body is rigid, and he somehow has managed to place his shoulder between the doctor and me so that I have to lean to make eye contact with the OB.

Dr. Cole frowns and studies the file in his hand. "Oh, my apologies, I must've…" He flips a page.

"No, it's okay. You're right." I squeeze Blake's hand. "Moorehead is my last name. I just…I'm changing it."

I plan on changing it to Daniels once we get married, but until then I wanted to have the same last name as my daughter. It sounds silly, what with Stew being a major grade-A fuckface, but with everything Axelle has gone through, changing my name felt like abandoning her.

The doctor grins again, his eyes moving between Blake and me and then to my ring finger. "For legal purposes, we'll need to keep Moorehead, but how about I call you Layla?" He gives me a kind and professional smile before scribbling something in my file.

My hand, pinched in Blake's tight grip, starts to ache.

"Two weeks until your due date." He puts down my file and washes his hands. "Are you having any issues you'd like to discuss, questions?"

I shake my head. "No."

Dr. Cole plops down on the rolling stool while Cassie takes his side next to a tray of supplies that from a quick glance only contains rubber gloves and lubricant. "If you could go ahead and lie back for me, pop your feet in the—"

"Whoa, whoa, whoa…hold on there, doc." Blake moves what seems like one step but places his entire body between the male doctor and me. "I hate to be a dick, but—"

"Blake!" I whisper-yell and hope my embarrassment and irritation at his behavior comes through. I love that Blake is protective, but this is the friggin' OB's office for crying out loud.

"Where's Dr. Evans?"

"Mr. Daniels, Layla's regular doctor is on call, so she's at the hospital, delivering a baby." Cassie's explanation is rushed, as if she senses the tick in Blake's time bomb. "I can assure you Dr. Cole will take good care of—"

"Oh"—a humorless chuckle rumbles in Blake's chest—"I'm sure he will."

I hook my fingers in his back belt loop and tug. "Stop it! You're being ridiculous."

Dr. Cole looks amused by Blake's outburst, which I know will only piss Blake off more. "I've been studying obstetrics and gynecology for over—"

"Yeah? Me too, but I didn't get a fancy degree. You go to school for what? Ten years to study pussy...as a dude? Yeah... no. You're not getting your fingers or eyes anywhere near my woman."

I groan and drop my chin to my chest. This is happening. Is this seriously fucking happening? I can't even raise my eyes to see the expressions on the doctor's and Cassie's faces, but their silence speaks volumes.

"Now, if you could please find a female doctor or nurse to check Layla, that'd be fan-fucking-tastic." He leans back so his butt hits my knees, creating a barrier between us while hiding my body. "We'll wait."

The warble of the rolling chair and shift in the tension tells me Dr. Cole has stood up. "I can't even imagine what you think my intensions are, but I'm a medical doctor and have been for five successful years. I've not given you a single reason not to trust me with—"

"You're a dude, right? Gotta dick? Those are my reasons. Unless you tell me now that you're gay, and from the looks of you I'd guess you're not, you need to find a female for this exam. Sorry, bro, but doctor or not, you're male, and no male is getting up close and personal with her."

"Oh my..." My face is on fire so much so that it starts to numb. "I can't believe this."

Without another word, the sounds of feet shuffling quickly and the door closing are the last things I hear before Blake's strong arms wrap around me.

"Don't hate me, Mouse. Please...I just can't sit here while any man puts his face between your legs."

I smack his side. "That was humiliating. He's a doctor." My body melts deeper into his while he runs his big hand through my hair in long and lazy strokes.

"I can't…I don't trust doctors, not anymore and not when it comes to you." There's a deep pain in his voice that shreds through my chest.

God, how could I forget? After Dr. Xavier put Blake's body through a living pressure cooker, pumping him so full of steroids he was crawling out of his skin, no wonder he's suspicious. Add to that his already fiercely protective and possessive nature makes his reaction completely understandable.

"Yeah." I nod into his chest.

"Promised I'd protect you and I am." He says it as if it's the simplest explanation. "I won't fail you again."

I want to smack him, to scream in his face that he didn't fail me. He'd had no control over his actions back then. I want to plead for him to understand that he saved me, but it's a tired conversation, and no matter how hard I try, he can never seem to forgive himself for what happened that night.

Silence hangs in the air, weighted with the memories of my past, a past I'd hoped I could move on from, but it hasn't been as easy as I thought. I don't hear Stewart's taunts anymore, but along with my pregnancy there've been nightmares. They could be flashbacks from the past, things I'd forgotten or repressed, but either way Blake has had a front row seat to them all.

I wrap my arms around his waist and feel the press of his lips to my head.

"No one gets to touch you unless I say it's okay, and Dr. Swinging Dick does not have my okay."

"Blake."

"What? Probably hits on half his patients." He mumbles that last bit as if to himself.

"His pregnant patients, I'm so sure."

"Don't care if he's a doctor. Pussy's pussy, and not a straight guy alive isn't turned on when he sees one."

I tilt my head back to meet his eyes and glare. "You did not just say 'pussy's pussy.'"

He shrugs. "I did, but yours is different."

I roll my eyes and shake my head, the warmth that his words conjured up earlier cooling quickly.

He tips my face up by my chin. "Yours is different because it's not just pussy anymore. It's mine."

The sincerity in his eyes, tick in his jaw, and grip of his fingers at the base of my neck are enough to bring tears to my eyes. I blink to stave them off.

"You get me?" His thumb rubs firmly along my lower lip.

I suck in a breath, aroused and so in love with the man before me. He's proven over and over that he'd do anything to protect me. I close my eyes and lean to rest my cheek to his chest. The paper gown I'm wearing opens completely so my bare belly presses firmly to his abdomen.

"Yeah, she gets me." He holds my head to his chest and drops kisses to my hair. "Love you, Mouse."

We sit in silence just holding each other when a small knock on the door announces what I hope to be a different and very female doctor.

"One sec," Blake calls and releases me. He takes a moment to close my gown over my breasts, my belly, and even tucks the edge over my thighs to protect my modesty. "Alright, come on in." He takes my hand in his and steps to the side of the exam table.

Cassie walks into the room first, followed by an older woman who's grinning. "Mrs. Daniels, I'm Patricia, the nurse practitioner. I'll be doing your exam today, and can I just say"—her eyes swing to Blake's—"I'll take good care of her."

Blake nods his approval, and I lie back, sighing in relief that, although being with this big strong fighter isn't free of its obstacles, I have no doubt that he'll always protect me.

Protect us.

Something we've never had before.

THREE

BLAKE

It's after twelve when I finally drag my ass to the training center. Once we got the news that Layla's dilated "at a two, thirty percent effaced, and cleared for a v-back," which basically translates into this baby could come at any time, I fed my woman and dropped her off at home.

She's still working with Cameron, but now that Eve is there to take over the majority of her duties, Layla has the option to come in or not, depending on how she's feeling. With Axelle in school, I figured this was a good time for her to have a quiet house and get some much-needed sleep.

As if on cue, a yawn claws its way up my throat. "Damn, who knew being pregnant would be so exhausting." I rub my eyes.

Jonah, Rex, and Mason are in various stages of eating or drinking shakes in the small break room. I rest my head in my hands, elbows propped on the table to support its weight.

"You think you're tired now, wait until you're up every two hours for feedings with a newborn." Jonah shakes his head, but can't hide that damn fatherly grin he's been sporting ever since Sadie was born. "You'd be surprised how quickly you get used to being barfed and pooped on by a tiny person."

Mason sets down his fork and groans. "Dude, do you mind?" He nods to his food. "No talk of shit and barf while I'm trying to eat."

Rex muffles his laughter and takes a huge gulp from his protein shake, clearly not at all affected by the conversation.

I tilt my head and study Jonah. How can he look so calm? He's more of a hothead than I ever was, and yet he's over there with a grin that would rival the Dalai Lama: all peace and harmony and not demonstrating even a sliver of the fear I can't seem to shake. Of course, he's not contending with a threat from the past in the form of a fucking email either.

"You guys know what you're having yet?" Rex pulls out a chair from the table, flips it around, and straddles it to prop his forearms on the back.

"Girl." It has to be because I can't raise a boy. The familiar panic I've been pushing down for the last nine months rushes to the surface.

"No kidding? A girl. Congratulations, man. Thought you guys wanted it to be a surprise." Jonah shoves a heaping spoonful of yogurt in his mouth.

"We do. That's what my gut tells me. We don't actually know for sure." As many times as I've tried to convince Layla that we should find out the sex, mostly so I could prepare, she's relentless and refuses. She says that she remembers the look on Jonah's face when he found out he had a little girl, and she wants to see the same expression on mine. Shit. I groan and rub my temples.

"What if it's a boy?" Rex shrugs, but his gaze is intent on me.

What if? Most likely I'll fuck the kid up just as my dad did me. I mean, what if my son ends up lying, being disrespectful, sneaking around, and doing shit I don't like…just as I did? A cold sweat breaks out over my skin, and I frantically search for a subject change. "You guys ever heard of a mucus plug?"

They all respond in some form of negative, and I explain what it is in graphic detail.

Mason shoves his food a good two feet from him. "You fucking asshole." He gags and swallows hard. "Got a fight coming up, and I need to eat to train, and you drop that kind of crap—" He gags again.

"That's fuckin' nasty." Rex laughs and downs the rest of his shake without even cringing.

Jonah plays with his yogurt, scooping spoonfuls and watching them plop back into the container, a look of disgust on his face. "I'm with Mason." He turns and tosses the half-eaten container into the trash. "That's disgusting."

"Oh, but puke and shit are okay." I shake my head and push up from the table. Talking about this crap isn't making me feel better. If anything, it only reminds me how unprepared I am for parenthood.

Why can't they all be as easy as Axelle? Yeah, she's dealing with shit, but at least we can talk it out. In a year, she'll be an adult and off to college. Easiest parenting gig ever.

"You ready?" I flick the back of Mason's head while moving past him to the training center.

I hear something hit the trash, probably his uneaten food. "Yeah, I'll take hits from you over this conversation any day."

—

LAYLA

I roll over and stare at my phone as it vibrates on the pillow next to me. I had it on the bedside table but got sick of reaching over to grab it every time it rang. I check the screen again.

Unavailable.

I send it to voicemail and drop it back to the pillow. Whoever has been calling me over these last couple days hasn't left a single message, and it's starting to creep me out. I considered talking to Blake about it, but he has enough on his mind as it is. I'm not even sure exactly what it is that has him acting so funny: not sleeping, spacing out in the middle of a conversation, and a general moroseness that is far from his normal easy-going attitude. In an attempt to pinpoint when his mood shifted, I track back week by week in my head. Christmas? Yeah, I'd say it was sometime around then, but why?

A long sigh falls from my lips, and I roll from my side to my back, kicking all the covers off and resting my hands on my pregnant belly.

"Sorry, little guy." I can't explain why I feel as if the baby is a boy, but I do. Maybe it's because Blake's such a powerful man—I can't imagine him producing anything but boys—or maybe it's wishful thinking. "No sleep for us." No matter how tired I am or how long I lie down with my eyes closed, I'm finding it harder and harder to sleep. I should clean something. Surely there's something in the house that needs to be sanitized…again.

I suppose I could drag my ass to the training center and do some busy work for Cameron. If nothing else, I'll get to hang out with Eve and lose myself in some effortless girl talk.

"Hey, Mama." Axelle pops her head in through the bedroom door, backpack slung over her shoulder.

I throw my legs over the side of the bed and push to sit up. My lungs crushed from the baby, I take a deep breath from the effort.

Her eyebrows pinch together. "You okay?"

"Yeah, I'm just waking up from a nap. How was school?"

She pushes into the room and drops down on the bed next to me. "Good. I aced my chem project. Looks like I'll be graduating and off to college after all."

There was some concern after everything happened and Stewart went to prison; Axelle's grades dropped dramatically.

The school threatened to hold her back if she couldn't pull them up, but thankfully she agreed to continue counseling and got a tutor.

"Proud of you, babe." I wrap my arms around her and kiss her temple. "Have you thought about where you want to go?"

She shrugs her backpack off and pulls a brochure out of the front pouch to hand it to me.

I take in the modern buildings, desert trees, and four bold letters. "UNLV?" I try to calm my voice even through my excitement.

Her gaze drops and a light pink colors her cheeks. "I want to stay close, ya know, just in case you need me to help out with the baby." She rubs her hand over my swollen belly with an expression of pure love lighting her bright blue eyes.

"Honey, you don't have to do that. I'll be fine. I have Blake, Raven, Eve and—"

"I want to." Panic flickers behind her eyes before it disappears and is replaced with worry. "I mean I hope that's okay with you."

"Of course it's okay." I run my hand through her long hair. "I just don't want you to give up any college experiences for babysitting."

She sighs, her eyes fixed on her baby brother or sister. "I'm just…I'm not ready to go too far yet."

I get that. I do. She has issues with abandonment for obvious reasons, and until she feels safe to swan dive from the nest, there's no way I'll push her out. "Good. You can come home for dinner on Sundays, and I'll do your laundry."

"Deal." She leans in and kisses my belly. "I have a study group at the library tonight, so I'll be home late."

"Okay, I'm going to the training center for a couple hours."

She walks out of the room, and for the second time today, my heart feels heavy with warmth. I have a man who loves me, a baby who'll be here any day, and a daughter who wants to hang around a little longer.

My phone vibrates again, and being lost in all the feelings tumbling though my chest, I don't think to check the caller ID.

"Hello?"

"L-Layla?"

My brows furrow at the unfamiliar male voice. I frequently get work-related calls from men, but there's something about the informal way he says my name that feels personal.

My back goes ramrod straight. "Who's this?"

"Please, just…don't hang up." He's whispering, jittery.

Adrenaline races through my veins, and my hand instinctively goes to my baby. "Who is this?"

"It was me that night…you got pregnant. I—"

I press End and toss the phone from my shaking hand. Whoever called was there that night? *It was me that night.* That makes him my rapist.

Oh no! No, no, no, this can't be happening.

Images from that night eighteen years ago flash through my mind. Whether they're actual memories or pieces of my nightmares, I don't know. My breath comes quickly, and I squeeze my eyes closed.

Bodies, confusion, they were laughing…

My stomach turns violently, and I race to the bathroom sink where I heave and spit but manage to keep from throwing up. Who the hell was that and how did he find me?

"I don't want this. I don't want this…not now." Not when everything in my life is finally good. Safe.

I take a deep breath and consider my reflection. Red-rimmed and watery eyes, pale skin, I swallow down some tap water and rinse my face. I'm not doing this. I refuse to allow whatever happened that night back into my life. No, I have control now. Total control. I breathe through the fear, in and out, until I'm back in command of my body. I'll be okay.

If I avoid his calls, he's sure to give up eventually. I have no desire to relive the night I got pregnant with Axelle, and she's made it clear she isn't interested in her biological father. End of story.

Rejuvenated, even if only a little, I brush my hair and throw on a pair of leggings, an oversized Henley that says "Rock n' Roll Stole my Soul," and my favorite biker boots. If nothing else, getting out of this house and around people will help.

I eye my phone on the bed as if it's a poisonous animal. "Don't be such a wimp, Layla." I grab it and shove it in my purse, vowing to only answer if I recognize the number and to make sure Blake doesn't catch wind of any of this.

I will protect my family, no matter the cost.

FOUR

LAYLA

"Here." Blake hands me two green pills and a glass of water then drops down beside me on the couch.

We'd just eaten dinner and settled in to watch "Vikings," which we'd DVR'd a few nights ago. It's the only show that we both agree kicks major ass, even if for completely different reasons. He likes the battle scenes, while I like watching Ragnar and Rolo do just about anything, preferably shirtless.

"Thanks." I throw back the pills and chase them down with a few healthy gulps of water. "You'd think after all this time I'd remember to take them."

He throws an arm over my shoulder, pulling me to the warmth of his side. "No need to remember when you got me, Mouse."

I wrap an arm around his firm middle and press my cheek to his chest, inhaling his masculine scent like pine trees after a long rain. It settles within and all around me, and I shove back the upsetting phone call from earlier. Whatever it is, I'll ignore it until it goes away.

Blake clicks the remote a few times. The only thing illuminating the dark room is the soft blue glow of the TV. Judging by last week's episode, I expect we'll start off with blood and bare-chested Vikings from the get-go. *Yay me!*

A twinge of arousal tingles between my legs. I expected sex to be the last thing on my mind when I was this far along in my pregnancy. I certainly don't remember being interested when I was pregnant with Axelle. Maybe the difference is Blake; he certainly throws off enough testosterone. I've also heard that women my age hit their sexual peak, and then there are all the hormones fighting for dominance and using my body as their battlefield. Funny, now that I think about it, I'm surprised I haven't chained Blake to the bed and used him as my personal sex slave for the last few months.

The visualization of my thoughts comes rushing in unbidden but *oh so* welcome: Blake's massive arms above his head, locked to the headboard as they ripple with tension to touch me, his abs flexing as he pulls at his restraints, and his teeth grinding as I drag my tongue down his neck. My thighs squeeze together, and I imagine the salty taste of his skin against my lips, the evidence of my attention to his body standing proudly and pressing into my hip.

A low moan slides its way up my throat.

"Damn, Mouse…they're not even doing anything but talking war strategy, and you're getting yourself all worked up." Blake adjusts his position on the couch, making no attempt to hide the bulge between his legs. "Can't fucking concentrate when you squirm against me, makin' that sound."

I tilt my head back to see the lust I feel reflected in his expression. "Can't help it. Something's wrong with me. I just… I'm…" I can't say it; it's too embarrassing.

"Horny." He lays it out so plainly I almost expect him to follow it up with a "Duh."

I cringe. That's such an unattractive word, but I guess it's the most accurate. "I think so, yeah."

Without another word, he hits pause, stands, and scoops me from the couch in a cradle hold. Even though I've gained thirty-five pounds, he still manages to handle me as if I weigh as much as a feather.

"You sure Axelle's gone 'til late?" he says with the guttural growl that drips off each word.

Excitement explodes in my belly, and I nod, absolutely frantic to get at him. I lean in and run my nose along his neck, taking what I can of him into my lungs. My tongue darts out to taste the powerful column of his throat. "I'm sure, but even if she comes home, I'll be extra quiet." I nip at his earlobe. A low groan vibrates his chest, and by some miracle of the pregnancy gods, I feel it between my legs.

"No way you'll be able to be quiet with what I'm about to do to your body." He places me gently on the bed then turns to shut and lock the door. When he whirls around back to me, his eyes have taken on a predatory glare, and his arms and shoulders bunch with feral anticipation. "Doc said no sex for six weeks after the baby comes. I plan on stocking you up with a lot of good orgasms before that."

He reaches behind his head and in one pull has his tee off and tossed aside. The dim light from the bedside table works to cast his muscles with dramatic shadows that only seem to make him look bigger, more menacing, and so fucking sexy. I suck my lip into my mouth to keep from begging him to hurry. My skin is hot and everything from my waist down throbs. I reach for the waistband of my yoga pants.

"Ah-ah-ah." He shakes his head slowly and wags one finger at the same pace. "I undress you."

With a flick of his hand, he pops the button on his jeans, and unzips them just enough to hang low, but not come off. My eyes dart to the deep vee of his muscles that disappears behind the denim, and I lick my lips to kiss him there, down lower. Hell, I'd cover every inch of his golden tan skin with my lips, twice if he'd let me.

One knee on the bed then the other, he moves to me and hooks the bottom of my sweatshirt. "Arms up."

I comply and close my eyes as he pulls the fabric up over my head so that my hair falls against my over sensitized and bare skin.

"Holy hell, woman."

I blink open at the mix of lust and appreciation I hear in his voice. His eyes are trained on my breasts, which are now two cup sizes bigger and braless, the way he likes them. His gaze rakes down over my belly, and a shiver slides down my spine to pool between my legs.

The lust I saw in his expression earlier dissolves into pure, raw admiration. "Most beautiful thing I've ever seen." He leans down, and his huge hands palm our baby beneath my skin. His lips dance over my belly, randomly dropping kisses and whispering words meant for only our child. Heat fires my eyes, and I fight to hold back the emotion that his gentle and reverent touch brings.

I fork my hands through his short hair, grabbing at strands, scraping my fingernails along his scalp, and holding him to me so desperately that I can't help but wonder if I'm hurting him.

He groans and uses his tongue to trace my belly button, which is no longer a deep hole, but is now punched out with the pressure of our growing child.

"Yes…" The word falls from my lips as I encourage him to go lower.

He smiles against me, clearly enjoying the way his attention has me writhing and wanton.

"It's not funny." The pulling ache of my body and the need to be filled completely by the man I love is painful. Tears spring to my eyes, but the slick wet feel of his tongue moving lower drowns my urge to cry.

"Always take care of you." His words are muffled against my skin, his tongue tracing along the dark line that leads from my belly button to disappear beneath my panties. He tugs at the elastic of my pants, but doesn't remove them, only goes lower until I feel the heat of his mouth exactly where I need him.

My fists grip the comforter, and I brace my feet against the bed to lift my hips, pressing into his mouth. He alternates between nipping and running the flat part of his tongue against the sensitive flesh.

Everything from my heart, my womb, between my legs, all of it throbs with the thunder of my pulse. I grab at his hair, push him down, press up, anything, but none of it is enough through my clothes.

A tiny noise, half growl, half whimper, rumbles from my lips before I give up. He chuckles, that sexy sound that would make a lesser woman fall to her knees and beg—is that not what I'm doing?

"Easy, Mouse…let me play." He continues his torture, raking his teeth along my inner thigh until my legs fall wide open. He pushes up to his knees, his hands gripping the outer part of my thighs, and gazes down at me. "How you could get more beautiful, I don't know, and yet you do."

Heat rushes to my cheeks. How can he see me as beautiful now? My breasts are bigger, but they look like road maps with the blue veins that've appeared with pregnancy, red jagged stretch marks on the sides of my hips ensure I'll be self-conscious in a bikini for the rest of my life, and I'm huge. Not everywhere, but if I give birth to less than a nine-pound baby, I'll be shocked.

As if he could read my mind, he dips down and kisses every mark, pushes up and palms my breasts, dragging his lips from one to the other and painting them with worshipful kisses. "Nothing sexier than seeing my baby growing big and strong inside the woman I love."

Another wave of sadness washes over me, and I want to cry. Stupid hormones. This is the way it's supposed to be, and it's so far from what I had when I had Axelle. I have to believe that even now our unborn child feels the love of his or her father and thrives from the warmth of his touch and comforting voice. Axelle never had that.

God, in what ways could that have affected her? If her biological father knew he had a daughter, would he be interested in her now? Could he make up for all she never had?

"Cut that shit out." The low grumble of Blake's voice followed by his firm grip on my thighs calls my eyes. He scowls down at me from his kneeling position between my legs. "Whatever you're thinking about, stop."

"What?" My act at nonchalance is a big fat fail, as his scowl grows tighter.

"Stay with me, here, not wherever you went in your head." His hands move down my thighs and hook the elastic of my pants.

"I'm here, Blake." The words fall from my lips on a whisper, and his biceps flex as he lifts my hips to remove my leggings and panties.

His gaze falls to between my legs and a moment of panic overtakes me. I haven't been able to actually see what things look like down there, but gauging from the flare of his eyes, I'd say it's not as bad as I imagine. He mumbles something about "dude doctors" that drips in sarcasm, and I stifle the urge to laugh. Just his eyes alone have my body so heated that I squirm in a silent plea for his touch.

His eyes move up and lock with mine, so green they look like fresh grass as they devour me. A tiny tick curls one side of his mouth before he pushes back to stand, drops his jeans, and kicks them to the side.

I sit up to my elbows and drink in a naked Blake: broad shoulders that cut into an equally wide chest and tapered abs that flow into the tight vee that leads to—*wow*. I bite my lip and push from my elbows to my hands; my mouth waters to taste him. He sees my hunger, recognizes it for what it is, and steps closer so that his knees hit the bed. I scoot, hang my legs over the edge straddling his and come face to face with his hard-on.

"Mmm..." I grip him and stroke.

His hands dive into my hair, pulling it back tightly so he can get a clear view of my lips. "Hell...you're killing me and you haven't even started."

Guiding him to my lips, I drown in the taste of Blake. My hands move around to his ass, tight and flexed so that the sides indent. I rake my fingernails across his cheeks and hold him to me.

A tiny tug on my hair and Blake does the moving for me. Swift grunts and long groans from his lips, I close my eyes and relax my throat. I don't have to see to know his abs are tight along with every other muscle in his towering frame. My body hums with power, the innate feeling of victory over a man like Blake Daniels as I sense his control waning.

Alternating long glides with short thrusts, he holds me captive by the hair at my nape, but runs his thumb in long soothing strokes up and down the side of my throat. "So good, perfect..." His words dissolve on a groan and his grip tightens before he rips himself from my mouth. Breathing heavily, he scoops one hand under each of my knees. With a gentle yank, I drop to my back, ass hanging off the edge of the bed, and he guides himself to me.

Before I started showing, he wouldn't enter me gently. He'd slam home, and I'd love every breathtaking inch, but, now, he wrangles the last bit of his control to enter my body in the sweetest and slowest way possible.

His eyes train on our connection. He pulls his lower lip between his teeth and pushes inside me. My legs instinctively wrap around his waist and lock behind his back, not because I'll fall if I don't, but to ground myself so he can use his hands freely. Moving with intentional strokes, he glides in and out while his hands, callused from lifting weights and playing guitar, run along the backs of my thighs.

"Blake…" The sensation of him filling me combined with the sweet way he's loving me coils deep in my belly, intensifying every stroke.

"Right here, baby." His fingers dig into my hips as if to punctuate his words.

"Kiss me."

The corner of his mouth lifts ever so slightly, as if his amusement isn't able to break through his lust. He leans over me, careful to brace his weight with his hands on the bed beside my head rather than collapsing on my body. He lowers himself in a push-up so his lips hover over mine.

I swallow every heated breath as he pants open-mouthed against my lips. I arch my back, searching for more and begging him to speed up. A slow shake of his head, side to side, and his lower lip drags against mine. "Ask me again."

"Kiss me, please."

He doesn't relent, but continues to torture me with his body, the tentative thrust of his hips and the barely there kiss. "Love you, babe. Love you so much."

My heart races with the heat of his words, and my tongue moistens my lips. His eyes move to my mouth and a low groan claws its way up his throat.

He's infuriating! Why won't he just kiss me?

I arch and roll my hips as best I can, using my feet against his ass as leverage. "Please…Snake."

His body stills, eyes flare, and he crashes his lips against mine. He swallows my gasp of pleasure and tangles his tongue with mine. We groan simultaneously, drinking from each other's mouths, and his pace quickens.

Before Blake, I never knew that it could feel like this. To open up my body to a man, pregnant and vulnerable, and know deep in my soul that he'd protect me, keep me safe, and die to do so. My legs begin to quiver with the effort it takes to hold him to me, and bolts of pleasure strike from my core. He breaks the kiss, pushes back and cups my ass to hold me, powering into me faster now, but still gently.

Tension pulls at my muscles, and my hands work to find a stronghold with the comforter because this orgasm is going to split me in two. I can't get enough air, and my back arches off the bed as I suck in one long final breath before the thunderous ecstasy rockets through my body. My muscles squeeze, as sensation rolls down my legs, arms, and up my neck until I'm dizzy. Floating back down, my body is a noodle, incapable of holding me up, not that I need to.

"Fuckin' hell, baby. Amazing…" His words drift into groans as he chases down his release. He drops down, arching his body over mine to suck one nipple deep into his throat and growls with a final thrust.

Heavy breaths, our bodies tacky with sweat, we stay like that: Blake's hands cupped at my backside, his big powerful body arched over me, cheek pressed to my chest. I run my fingers through his hair and grin at his responding shiver.

"I love you. You're amazing, always so gentle with me."

He turns his face to kiss my chest then slides his hands up my back to scoot me onto the bed fully and keep our connection. "Our baby is growing in this hot little body, Mouse. Of course I'm going to be gentle." He pulls out and drops to the bed beside me, gathering me in his arms so that my pregnant belly presses against his side.

I lay my hand flat against his chest, right over his heart where it thunders against my palm, warming me further. "Remember what the doctor said? Sex could induce labor."

"Yeah, hope you're not saying you wanna stop, because six weeks without being with you after this baby is born will probably kill me. Not at all interested in giving you up until I'm forced to by orders."

I draw figure eight patterns through his six-pack and grin as his goose bumps chase the path of my fingertip. "It's been so long since I've felt safe. At times like this, when we're alone and I'm wrapped in your arms, it feels like nothing could touch me. Like the world could end all around us and I'd be shielded from it."

Blake tenses at my side.

I don't know where that came from; the words just came tumbling out. It wasn't so much a conscious thought, just a random string of whatever was going through my head. "I know, it sounds crazy," I say suddenly feeling self-conscious.

I glide my hand back up to his chest and relax at the steady beat of his heart, fearing I'd find it racing even faster than before.

"Blake, if there's—"

My phone rings from my purse, which is sitting on the dresser across the room.

He taps my hip for me to move. "I'll grab it."

"No, wait." I hold on to him tighter.

He peels my fingers away from his ribs and moves to stand. "Let it go to voicemail. I want to talk to you—"

Before I can finish my sentence, he's up and heading to my purse. "Could be Axelle."

He's right, but my guess is his wanting to grab the phone has more to do with our conversation than it does Axelle's safety.

I study his naked backside while he fishes out my phone, and lick my lips as the stir of arousal pulls at my belly. Jeez get a grip! This must be what it feels like to be a teenage boy.

He turns around and I suck in a breath. His front is even more impressive than his back, but my perusal is short-lived when I notice he's glaring at my phone.

Oh crap.

FIVE

BLAKE

Four missed calls since before dinner, all from Unavailable. I hit the phone history and see the word Unavailable listed at least twenty times. Can't say I'm too upset about this particular call though. It saved me from having to look Layla in the eye again and tell her everything is okay when it sure as shit is not.

"This the telemarketer who's been calling?" I scroll down and see that whoever this is calls in spurts. Over and over before giving up for hours. All of the calls are listed as "missed."

"Oh, yeah…" She pulls her sweatshirt over her head. "I think so, but I don't know. I send it to voicemail, but they don't leave messages." She's searching for her pants, but I get the strangest feeling that she's avoiding my eyes.

"You've never answered." It's not a question as I can clearly see all the calls are listed on her phone in red…oh, except one. I hit the "I" for info on the call. Forty-seven seconds. She answered the phone and spoke to someone for almost a minute?

"No, never." She has her back towards me as she pulls her hair up into a ponytail. "It's a UFL-issued phone; it could be anyone. If it were important, they'd leave a message."

Why, my little Mouse, what are you hiding?

"Huh." I toss the phone back into her purse, and my mind races as I pull on my jeans and throw my tee into the dirty clothes hamper. "Maybe next time just answer; see what they want."

I pin her with a stare and watch her squirm, which confirms my conclusion.

"Yeah, uh...good idea."

What the fuck? Chances are this is nothing, but what kind of nothing is important enough to not share with me? My internal question is followed by a wave of shame. I haven't told her about the email, but it's only because I don't want her to worry. Is it possible she's hiding something from me for the same reason?

"Baby?"

"Hm?" She blinks up at me.

Giving her one more chance to come clean, I pin her with a stare. "You sure you have no idea who's calling? You never answered any of these calls?"

Seconds tick by, before she rolls her shoulders back and stands tall. "I did once, on accident, but no one was there." She shrugs, her too-cool demeanor seeming more like a smoke screen.

"Right." I can't take my eyes off her, and something tugs in my chest: worry, fear, anxiety. "Love you."

She smiles and closes the space between us. Her belly presses between my hips as she pushes up on her tiptoes and drops a kiss to my lips. "I love you too, Blake. So much."

She dips her chin and walks away.

"Mouse, hold up—" My phone rings in my pocket, AC/DC's "Back in Black" as the ringtone. "What the...?" I hit Accept. "Brae, man, what's up?"

"Dude, where the fuck are you, asswipe?"

"Nice to hear from you too, dick." A tiny grin pulls at my lips, hearing my little brother's voice.

"I've been knocking on your door for-fuckin'-ever. Your car's in the spot, but—"

"Oh shit, you're here?" I move out of my bedroom and down the hallway to the front door.

"No, man, I'm in China, fuckhead." He huffs out an irritated breath. "I'm standing outside your—"

I swing open the door to see my brother wearing his military-issued green tee shirt and fatigues. He's got the phone to his ear, and he's scowling. "'Bout time. Shit." He hits a button on his phone and drops it into his pocket.

I do the same. "What the hell are you doing here?"

"You gonna invite me in?" He holds his arms out. "Freezin' my dick off out here."

"Of course." I step back and open the door for him. "Small things freeze easily. Come on in."

He passes by me with a shove to my chest and a mumbled "asshole."

"Braeden?" Layla calls from the kitchen and moves toward us with a bottled water in hand. "What're you doing here?" Her bright smile and freshly-fucked blush make her even more gorgeous than she already is.

My kid brother's eyes brighten a little, and I can tell he notices it too. "Hey, little sister, you look amazing. Ready to pop, but amazing." He hooks her over the shoulder, and she leans in for an awkward side hug.

"I love that you call me little sister when I'm almost old enough to have birthed you." She grins up at my over-six-foot-tall brother and then claims her position at my side.

Brae's eyes move between us, taking in my shirtless torso, her sated expression, and my unbuttoned jeans. "Ah, that's why you didn't hear me knockin'."

"Servicing my woman, bro. Pregnancy makes her demanding."

Layla's eyes bug out of her head and she gasps. "Blake!"

Brae rubs his mouth, trying to hide his grin. "Fuckuva job, dude. I can see by your shit-eating grin it's makin' you miserable."

"Oh my God, I'm outta here." Layla kisses my jaw then whirls red-faced to head to the bedroom. "You guys have fun. Goodnight!" Her farewell is called over her shoulder with a tiny wave of her hand before she disappears into the room and closes the door.

I catch Brae's eyes fixed down the hallway, a big smile on his face, before he meets my glare. "She looks hot, dude. Still tiny as hell, but with bigger boobs."

I smack him upside the head. "Eyes to yourself." Despite my irritation, I can't help but grin at my brother, knowing he's pushing my buttons and missing our verbal spars. "You want a beer?"

"Yeah, that'd be great."

We move into the kitchen, and I pull two Coronas from the fridge, poppin' the tops, and slide one to my brother, who has taken a seat at the island. "So what's up? What brings you to Vegas? Someone die?" I'm half joking. The fact is it's hard for Brae to get time off for trips, and my dad would have to approve of this visit, which means he's here on a mission from The General.

He shrugs, takes a long pull off his bottle, and then fixes his eyes on mine. "Had a few days off. Wanted to get off the reservation."

He's lying. "You need a place to crash? Axelle's got the guest room now, but you're welcome to crash on the couch in the music room."

"Nah…thanks though. I'm staying on the strip." He leans back and locks his hands behind his head. Fuck, but the dude has doubled in size since I last saw him.

"Save money if you stay with us."

"True but"—a slow smile spreads across his face—"can't bring chicks home to fuck at my brother's house with his teen-age daughter and pregnant fiancée in the next room."

I cringe at the thought of random bitches in my house with my girls. Raising my bottle to my lips, I nod. "Good point."

We sit in silence and sip our beers, and I can't shake the feeling that he's here for more than a friendly visit. "How're things on base?"

"Mm. Same." His gaze darts around the room.

What the fuck. "Brae, man. Out with it." My brother has never hid shit from me before; whatever he came to Vegas to say seems to be difficult.

"Don't shoot the messenger, man."

Beer churns in my gut. I knew it. "Deliver it already."

He spins the bottle in slow circles. "They want you to come home."

"Excuse me?" My parents have never asked me to come home for a visit. My mom claims it's because I'm too busy, but we both know the truth. I can't be around my dad for more than twenty-four hours without getting into a fight with him.

"You heard me. They're requesting your presence." He drags out the last three words, making it sound even more ridiculous than it already is.

"Why?" A humorless laugh burst from my lips.

"If I could tell you, brother, they wouldn't be asking to see you in person."

I shake my head. "I can't, man. Layla's due any day. No way I'm leaving her."

He nods, but it's halfhearted. "Sure, sure, I understand, but"—he sets his eyes, so identical to mine it's freaky, on me—"it'd just be a day trip: flight in the morning, be home that night."

"No way, I'm not leaving Layla." Why do I sound so defensive as if he's going to drag me home against my will? "I can't believe after all these years they want me home and I'm supposed to jump at the sound of their whistle?"

He keeps his mouth closed, listening.

"I mean, come on, Brae. They haven't had anything to do with me in years."

"It's not really Dad, bro. It's Mom. She sent me."

I blink and try to figure out if I just hallucinated. My mom doesn't even piss without my dad's say-so. What could possibly be so important that she'd need to see me in person? No, it doesn't matter. "I love Mom, I do, but my priorities are my family." I point toward the hallway. "Layla and Axelle are my family."

I don't miss the flash of disappointment in his eyes and a strange tension pulls tight between us.

"Dude, you're family too, but you know what I mean."

"Sure, yeah." He nods and takes a long swig of his beer. "Thing is…this is kinda important. It's one day; you don't have to stay the night. One day."

My eyebrows drop low as realization dawns. "Hold up…so you know what this is all about?"

He shifts uncomfortably in his seat. "I do."

At least he didn't try to lie.

"Just tell me what's going on." In the short amount of time I wait for him to answer, I review every possible scenario in my head. Maybe they're moving, Dad's retiring, or maybe now that I'm having a baby, they're ready to mend fences.

How would I deal with the possibility of them wanting to be grandparents? I wish I could let the past die a cold miserable death, but the resentment that ignites in my gut proves the past is alive and kickin'.

I can't handle the thought of my dad treating my kids the way he did me, ignoring our feelings and subjecting us to a military upbringing. My fists clench, and the beast that raged when Gibbs had me drugged reminds me how easy it was to act just like my father. Reminded me how close I am, how vulnerable I am to becoming exactly like him.

No, the safest thing I can do for my family, for Layla, Axelle, and our baby is to stay the fuck away from my parents.

"I'd tell you if I could, but I can't. Promised Mom I'd let her talk to you."

"Just fuckin' tell me. No, you know what?" I chuck my bottle top into the garbage so hard it hits with a satisfying thud. "Fuck it. I don't care."

What could my mother possibly have to say to me now? After everything we've gone through, the silence between us over the past…way too fuckin' long. She's married to a man who despises me and has never had shit to say until now? Years of resentment resurface and my skin pricks with irritation. My fingers flex and itch to get at Layla, to bury myself inside her and work off the anger while reminding myself what matters. But anger-fucking my nine-month pregnant woman isn't in the cards.

A heavy session in the music room oughtta do it.

"Sleep on it."

I hear the sound of the key in the front door and breathe deeply to calm my nerves. "Axelle, come here for a sec."

The sound of her dropping her backpack on the tile echoes through the room before Braeden catches sight of her and stands.

"Hey, Brae! What's up?" She gives my brother a hug.

"Damn, short stuff! You look like you're old enough to be hittin' the bars." He playfully pulls her knit beanie down over her eyes.

"Ha, barely." She pushes the hot pink material back off her forehead. "But"—she holds up one finger—"I'm *almost* old enough to legally buy cigarettes."

"You better not." I growl and glare at my teenage daughter.

She rolls her eyes and shakes her head then moves around the island to the fridge and pulls out some kind of diet soda shit. "How long are you here for?"

Braeden shrugs and his eyes dart to mine, communicating that his stay depends on how long it takes for him to convince me to go home.

Plan on an extended stay, brother.

"Not sure yet."

"Cool! We'll have to barbeque or something while you're in town." She takes a swig of her drink then eyes me. "Where's Mom?"

"Bedroom. How was your study group?"

"Good, I think I'm ready to ace this exam. Killian is a whiz at math. I swear he's like a modern day Carl Gauss."

Braeden swings his gaze to me, his eyebrows dropping low, then slides it back to her. "Who the fu—er…crap is Carl Gauss?"

She looks at me, blue eyes sparkling.

"No." I shake my head and take a swig of my beer. "Don't look at me. I have no friggin' clue who he is either."

She rolls her eyes and drops a hip onto a barstool. "Does 'It is not knowledge, but the act of learning that grants the greatest enjoyment' sound familiar?"

My brother and I lock eyes for a second, and I can see the confusion I'm feeling reflected in his expression. We both give our version of negative grunts.

"Huh…" She giggles. "Did you guys graduate from high school?"

Her little jab has Brae grinning and pride swelling in my chest. I love that she's brave, strong enough to throw sass, and not afraid to express herself. Just like her mom.

"Ah…I know who Carl Gauss is." Brae locks his arms behind his head. "He's the beer guy. Pretty good stuff too."

She laughs and shakes her head. "No, he's a mathematician. Killian talks about him a lot. I think he's like, I don't know, his idol or something." Her hands shove deep into the pockets of her sweatshirt, and I know she's saying something without using words. I just can't figure out what it is. My guess is it has something to do with Killer.

He and Axelle have been friends for a while, but it's obvious the young fighter-in-training has feelings for her beyond friendship. Her feelings for him are more of a mystery, and I can only hope that one day she'll figure her shit out and give the guy a chance. That is, after I put the fear of God into the kid that he'll be keeping his dick to himself until she's...well, forever.

"As much as I love a good ole conversation about dead mathematicians, I've been stuck on base with a bunch of dudes for way too long and the city waits." Brae stands and throws back the rest of his beer. "I'm off to break some hearts." He gives us a half-hearted salute. "I'll touch base with you guys tomorrow, and we can figure out our plans for Axelle's barbecue."

Axelle squeals and scurries over to give Brae one last hug. "Awesome, see you then." Her eyes find mine. "I'm going say goodnight to Mom."

I nod and she takes off to my room before I turn to my brother.

"Thanks for the beer."

"Of course." I move around the island to walk him out.

Once at the door, he pauses and meets my eyes. "Do me a favor? Just think about it. Mom really wants—"

"Have fun tonight." I can't help it. I just don't want him to finish that sentence. Whatever Mom really wants is only going to fuck with my head. The fact is I can't leave, not even for a day.

Understanding washes over his expression, and his jaw clenches before he pushes whatever it is he's thinking down and relaxes his shoulders. "Right." He moves to the door.

"Don't do anything I wouldn't do."

He chuckles and smirks at me from over his shoulder. "Oh, so don't…" He scratches his jaw in thought. "Huh, I guess anything goes then."

I shove him through the front door, and even though it was an easy shove, it doesn't faze him. I remind myself to ask him later what he's benching. Later, when the request from my mom isn't burning a hole in my head.

What the hell could she possibly have to say now? And why do I even care?

SIX

LAYLA

It's cramped and dark. I can't straighten my legs or maybe it's just that I don't have the strength to. My head spins and I try to focus on where I am.

Voices. Laughter and whispering jumbled together.

My legs move, but not by my will. They're being moved for me. I struggle to slam them closed but lack the strength and muscle control. They fall open.

Something tells me I should fight, but I don't. I'm numb. Not only physically, but mentally. Detached and floating beyond my body.

Where am I?

I'm pulled on, rubbed against. My mouth is wet and warm. I gag uncontrollably and try to turn my head away.

"Shit, she's waking up!"

That voice…so familiar and yet…not.

I push back the haze and reach for consciousness. It's within my reach. I can feel it. Cold air hits my bare body and pulls me closer to the surface.

Feeling returns in my feet, hands; my heart pounds in my chest. I blink open my eyes only to recoil.

Blake!

His hand at my neck.

His angry glare, dark with hate, fixes on mine.

I can't breathe! I gasp and try to rip at his arm, but I'm frozen inside my body. I can't scream, can't fight, and succumb...

"Oh God!" I gulp air and shoot straight up in bed. My body is tangled in the sheets. Sweat dampens my tee, and I smooth back the hair stuck to my face. What the hell...another nightmare. They're so vivid it's like living through it all over again, but with more clarity.

I reach over to find Blake, to curl up in his arms and let his strength chase away the terror, but my hand hits the pillow. The sheets are cold and I check the clock.

"Four a.m." He hasn't been to bed yet?

Last night after I left him and Braeden to their boy talk, I watched TV in bed and talked to Axelle. By the time she went to bed, I could hear the faint guitar sounds coming from Blake's music room. I wasn't sure if he was in there with his brother or by himself, but either way I didn't want to interrupt.

Has he been in there all night?

I push up and slide from the bed, making sure my tee is pulled low just in case Brae is still here. The door to the music room is closed, but not locked. I push it open and hit a wall of dark. Maybe he's not in here? I flick on the light switch and a soft smile pulls at my lips.

Blake's asleep on the couch, his arm behind his head, the other resting at his chest, one long powerful leg cocked and leaning against the back of the couch while the other hangs off the side. The sofa looks tiny in comparison to his huge body.

With timid steps so that I don't wake him, I move to the edge of the couch and squat down close to watch him sleep. He seems so innocent now. No cocky grin or sexy dirty talk sliding from those lips. No, now they carry innocence. Full, kissable, and parted slightly as he breathes deeply. His eyes, usually full of mischief and insinuation are now closed, long dark eyelashes splayed across his olive-skinned cheeks. He's so handsome it almost hurts.

I take a second to consider what parts of him our baby will get. Boy or girl, it doesn't matter. He or she will be beautiful carrying his genes. A slow sigh falls from my lips, and I bite my lip to avoid any other noise that might wake him. He remains still, his breathing steady.

Unable to keep from touching him, I trace his full lower lip with my fingertips and moan as the simple act unfurls a flurry of desire to feel his lips on me. So soft—he shifts slightly and I hear the sound of crinkling paper. Leaning in, I see the corner of an email peeking up from between his body and the back cushion of the couch.

I pull on it, eyes squinting since I'm not wearing my glasses, and read the subject. "Anonymous inquiry into birth records."

His hand shoots out, grabs my wrist, and yanks hard.

"Ow!" I let go of the paper.

His eyes fly open. "Shit!" Stunned, he drops my arm and throws both hands into the air. "Fuck, Mouse, are you okay?" He moves to touch me, but something he sees in my expression makes him recoil.

"I'm okay. I am." I force a nervous laugh. "Just scared me, but I'm fine." *That fucking dream!*

"No, it's not okay. You look scared out of your damn mind. What did I do?" He blinks through sleep-fogged eyes, but I can hear the self-hatred in his voice.

I lean in and grab his face, forcing his eyes to mine. "You didn't do anything. I had a bad dream. I was already shaky, and then I snuck up on you."

"I hurt you."

"No, you just spooked me." I lean in and drop a soft kiss on his lips. "I shouldn't have messed with you in your sleep."

Shame washes over his expression, and I hate myself for making him feel bad. "Damn, I was out of it."

"You needed your sleep." My eyes dart to the paper that's wedged between Blake and the couch. "What is that?"

His body tenses. "Hm?"

"That paper?" I motion to it with a nod.

"Oh, um…" He reaches over, pulls it out, and rather than showing it to me, he folds it up and shoves it into his pocket. "It's nothing, just some leftover ends to tie up with my adopting Axelle."

I stare at him, waiting for him to meet my eyes, but he doesn't. I have no reason to doubt him, but something doesn't feel right. I slide a strand of my hair between two fingers and twirl. "What kind of leftover ends? I thought it was all pretty cut and dry." He doesn't answer, and panic speeds my breathing. "Blake?"

He exhales hard and drops his head. "Dammit…fuck."

My nerves, already shot from my nightmare and jumpy from waking Blake, vibrate with panic at the defeat I hear in his voice. "What?"

He rubs his eyes with one hand. "I was hoping…shit."

I crawl up onto the couch, and he shifts to sit up next to me. "What the hell is going on, Blake?" My stomach somersaults.

He reaches into his pocket and pulls out the paper then sets his worried eyes on mine. "I was hoping to keep this from you until I figured out what it means."

My eyes widen. "Blake, you can't keep anything from me, especially if it's about Axelle!"

He cringes and I rip the folded up paper from his hands.

"I just want to keep you safe and the baby safe. I didn't want you to get upset…" He continues to talk as I unfold the single page email that's from the Las Vegas Police Department.

Blake,

As per your request, I'm notifying you that, on December 21st, the birth records of Axelle Rose Moorehead were requested by someone in Spokane, WA acting under "Anonymous." That same day the individual also requested the divorce records of Layla Marie Devereux.

That is all the information I have for you at this time.

Det. Dave Hodgeson

Las Vegas Police Department

My pulse thunders in my ears, my hand shakes, and I can't seem to focus enough to ask one of the many questions swirling through my head.

"I've had Dave keep an eye on things for me, just for a little while. After Stew went to prison, I worried he had someone out there, a silent partner who might go sniffing around. I honestly didn't think Dave would find anything, but…"

A dull ache forms between my eyes. *Unavailable.* "Do you think it has something to do with…with…" I can't say it, but a look of understanding washes over his face.

"I don't know, Mouse, but I don't want this shit hitting us out of the blue when we're not expecting it. 'If you want peace, prepare for war.' Remember? I was keeping my finger on the pulse just in case, and thank God I was." He cups my face, forcing my eyes to lock with his. "Whatever happens, we'll be ready."

"If it's someone from my past, what could they possibly expect to gain from birth records and divorce records?" I guess it's possible that Stew has his lawyers working on something, but I'm not as worried about that. The police have his confession, so he'll be locked in jail until Axelle is grown and has a family of her own. But, if *anonymous* and *unavailable* are the same then…A flash of my nightmare has me curling into Blake.

"So what now?" I hand the email back to him, and he folds it up and shoves it into his pocket.

"Now, you go back to takin' care of yourself and our baby while I take care of this."

I grip his knee, imploring his eyes. "Blake, I want—"

"No." He pins me with a powerful glare. "No one will get near you or Axelle, do you hear me? You focus on getting this baby here whole and healthy, Axelle focuses on getting into UNLV and what new music she wants to download, and I take care of this."

I blink a few times, considering how best to respond. Fact is he'd be insane to think I'm going to stay out of this. I'll always protect my family. "Alright." I nod and knot my fingers together in my lap, hoping he doesn't see my lie.

"Alright?" His unbelieving tone followed by silence calls my eyes to his.

"Yeah." I shrug.

He narrows his glare. "Alright."

He doesn't believe me, but he can't prove I'm lying, so I just nod and flash a shy smile.

"I'm tired." I stand and hold out my hand. "You ready for bed?"

He takes it. "Yeah, babe." A long yawn crawls from his throat.

I pull to get him to stand, but he doesn't budge. "Are you comfortable here?"

He tugs me to his lap and wraps his body around mine. It's weird because, being in his lap, I should feel like the one being held, but the way his arms are wrapped around my belly, his head to my chest, it's as if I'm holding and comforting him. "No. I want to be in bed with you."

I run my hand through his hair and kiss his head. "You okay?"

He grunts his "yes," but doesn't lift his head.

"You sure?" As disturbing as the email is, it only manages to light a fire in my gut to protect those I love. Blake can do what he thinks he needs to, but I'll do what I can to end this before the demons from my past come back to haunt us.

"Take me to bed, baby." God, why does he sound so desperate? I don't know what to do or what to say, but every cell in my body wants to take away the pain I hear in his voice.

"Okay." I push up and take his hand, leading him to our bed. He shucks his jeans and boxer briefs and my mouth instantly waters. He pulls my shirt, but leaves my panties in place and crawls into bed, taking me with him.

Pulling my back to his front, he palms my breast and buries his nose in the back of my neck. "I'll never lose you."

That's what he's afraid of? "Never."

"I'd die without you." His hand rubs my belly. "All three of you."

I reach over my shoulder and cup the back of his neck. "We're not going anywhere."

He flexes his hips into my ass, and I can feel what the proximity of our bodies is doing to him. A low moan vibrates in his chest, but rather than instigate love making, he only pulls me closer until his breathing evens out.

He's asleep.

I sink into his hold and close my eyes, knowing that I won't sleep. The dreams...the detective's email...rolling it around in my head makes me feel dizzy, as if I'm falling.

Blake's arms close around me even tighter, and I visualize that he's holding me together, keeping me grounded, until the drop feels more like floating.

SEVEN

BLAKE

Throwing open the doors of the training center first thing in the morning, I already feel a fraction better than I did last night. The list of things that calm my inner turmoil is short: Layla, music, and beating the shit out of something.

It took me over an hour in my music room to work off the pent up frustration from all my unanswered questions. I fell into a restless sleep after that, only to wake up to a terrified Layla, who looked like an animal that had been beaten. And when shit can't get worse, it usually does. She spotted the email.

Talking to her about it loosened some of the tightness I've been carrying in my chest, and her response was not what I'd expected. I'd anticipated her reaction since I received the damn thing, and I would've sworn she'd have been out for blood. Instead she agreed to leave the whole damn thing to me. The victory I felt was short-lived once my brain kicked in and reminded me that nothing with Layla has ever been that easy.

"Mornin', Blake." Vanessa, the training center's receptionist and huge pain in my ass, bats her eyelashes in greeting.

I ignore her stupid attempt at flirting. "Vanessa, heads up, my brother Braeden's coming in this morning."

I texted Brae right when I woke up and invited him down for a tour and a workout. He's never been to the UFL facility before, and I figured working out would be a good excuse to get him alone. If he'd just fucking tell me what's going on at home, I could tell my parents to go to hell and get back to worrying about more important things: like the fact that someone's after information on my woman and daughter.

I roll my head to relieve the tension. "When he gets, here if you could show him back—"

"He's already here." Her eyebrows pop up and a flicker of female appreciation lights her expression. "If I'd known there was a younger, sexier version of you out there, I would've been nicer to Layla after she claimed you."

"Sexier? Yeah right." I roll my eyes at Vanessa's blatant attempt at getting me riled. As if I give a flying fart what she thinks of me, Layla, or my brother. "Where's he at?"

"I left him with Jonah." She jerks her head toward the hallway with a flick of her reddish-blond hair. "They're in the gym."

I mumble a quick "thanks" and head off to find him.

Once inside the warehouse-like facility, I spot Jonah and Braeden by the octagon. Their attention is on two fighters sparring inside. As I draw closer, I recognize them as Rex and Mason.

I shove my brother from behind. "What up, dicklick?"

He stumbles one step, groans, and rubs his temples. "Hungover, please whisper."

"Idiot." I shake my head and give Jonah a chin lift before joining them to watch Rex and Baywatch. "Damn, that kid's fast."

Jonah's arms are crossed over his chest, his gaze focused as he studies the fighters. "Yeah, Rex isn't even taking it easy on him anymore. Baywatch is a fuckin' animal in there."

I nod and watch as Mase gets Rex into full mount position so quickly the tattooed fighter barely has time to register what happened, much less block it.

No one talks about it, but we all know where Mason's extra drive to kill is coming from. Eve's choosing Cameron over Mase lit a fire to annihilate in the kid's ass. He came to Vegas all wide-eyed and innocent. Now the guy takes the asshole ranks. He's pissin' people off, getting reprimanded for talking shit to other fighters, even got suspended for a bar fight.

I don't judge him. Hell, if Layla had ended up leaving my ass for another guy, I'd be in prison for murder.

Just then Mason gets Rex in a ground guillotine choke. We all step closer to the cage.

"Sweet move, Baywatch!" Jonah grips the chain link, calling into the training fighters. "Rex, tap!"

Rex taps, as he should. The hold he's in is next to impossible to break, and we're not here to kill each other.

Mase tightens the hold, his teeth bared. *Fuck.* My eyes dart to Jonah, who has his gaze focused on Mason's arm.

"Mase, let up!"

He doesn't. Rex's muscles go limp, but regain and struggle. Fuck, he's going unconscious. I hook a foot and climb the fence just as Jonah does the same. Within seconds, we're at Mason.

Jonah wraps one arm around the front of Mason's neck as if he's a feral dog. "Let up! Now!"

I hook Rex under the arms, and the second Mase gives in to Jonah's command, I pull Rex back and set him on his ass to recover.

"What the fuck, Baywatch?" I get in the punk's face and ready for him to take a swing. Hell, I walked in here looking to burn up some energy. Weights would do the job, but I'd much rather beat someone's ass. "You try that shit again, I will end you, you understand?" I shove him back and he drops his chin, breathing hard.

"You're done for the day. Pack your shit, go home, and calm the fuck down." Jonah doesn't waste another word on the kid and moves to check on Rex, who has a huge fucking grin on his face.

"That was epic." He pushes up, heads over to Mase, and grabs him by his headgear. "Good job, man. No hard feelings."

Baywatch shakes his head and has the decency to appear ashamed. Good little shit. "Sorry, man. I'm…fuck…that was uncool. I'm sorry." He offers his fist to Rex, who fist bumps him back.

Better man than I. Although, it wasn't too long ago I was all juiced up and had no idea and pulled something similar with Rex.

"Rex, our resident punching bag." I motion to him and he takes a dramatic bow.

"At your service," he says with a bloodied-lip grin.

We all laugh, the tension in the air dissolving enough that we move to get on with what we came here for.

I hop the octagon fence and give my brother a shove. "Show's over; let's hit some weights."

He follows me toward the weight room. "Dude, that was kickass. I can see why you like it here. I mean I get to train, but we never get good hand-to-hand like what I just saw there."

Poor guy never has been sent to the war he's training for day in and day out. I remember what it was like to know so much and have to bottle it up, never given the opportunity to exercise my training in a physical and tangible way.

I flick on the lights and hit the stereo, putting Black Sabbath on Pandora to make sure plenty of hard metal pumps through the room and keeps us energized. We hit the free weights first, and I realize immediately that my baby bro has been spending plenty of time in the gym. He needs zero instruction as we move mindlessly through our own workouts, grabbing weights similar to what I lift.

He fatigues quicker than I do, but that could have a lot to do with his extracurricular activities. As much as I enjoyed living that life when I did, I'm glad it's part of my past. I push him to hit the bench press, and after a few sets, we take a water break.

"How's the hangover now?" I toss him a towel that he immediately presses to his face.

"Much better," he says, out of breath. "Thanks for asking me down here. I'd probably be nursing this hangover with a little hair of the dog in the casino if you hadn't texted me." He takes a swig of water. "Also helped me get rid of my date from last night."

Well, I'll be damned. My baby brother's got game.

"Careful, dude. Vegas chicks aren't like the chicks back home."

He glares up at me. "Why not? I mean pussy's pussy."

I drop my chin and laugh at how he sounds just the way I did the other day at the OB's office. I take a minute to imagine the heaping pile of verbal comebacks my Mouse would lob at Brae if she were to hear him say that. Damn, I love that woman.

"I'm just warning you now not every girl is as innocent as she might pretend to be. 'Lotta pros in Vegas."

He lifts one eyebrow. "You mean prostitutes?"

I wipe the back of my neck with the towel. "No, not necessarily, but professional manipulators that prey on pretty boys like you." He throws his sweaty towel at me, and I swipe it out of the air before it hits my face. "Just be safe, that's all I'm sayin'."

He recoils, his lips twisted as if he's tasting something he doesn't like. "Please, tell me this isn't the you-better-be-using-protection talk. Got that from Mom at fourteen."

"Yeah? From Mom? I never got that talk."

He shrugs. "That's because you were too busy running off to play piano when you were fourteen. I was going to the senior prom with 'Kitty Cat' Coffman when I was fourteen." His eyes go unfocused and he grins. "Never heard a woman purr before, but damn…" He shakes his head.

"You fucked 'Kitty Cat' Coffman?" That girl was gorgeous and four years older than him. "She was in my grade."

"What can I say, brother?" He swipes a pretend piece of lint from his shoulder. "Hate the playa' not the game."

"Dude, never say that again." I toss my sweaty towel in his face. "You sound like a douchebag."

"Whatever, I appreciate your concern, but I'm a big boy." He chuckles and pushes up from the bench. "At least, that's what she said."

My jaw falls open on its hinges. "How dare you? That's my line."

He laughs and pulls his elbow over his head to stretch his triceps. "Your concern for me is sweet, but I can take care of my own dick, thank you very much."

I bite down against the urge to tease him about taking care of his own dick and focus on what I asked him down here for.

"So Mom wants you to bring me home to share some big secret with me, huh?" I busy myself by sliding plates off the bar and racking them.

"I don't see what the big deal is. Just go home, let her say her peace, and then you can come back to your *perfect* life." He shrugs, but I can see the frustration working in his expression.

My hands freeze on the weights. "What the hell's that supposed to mean?"

"Nothing." He chugs down the rest of his water and tosses the empty bottle in the nearby trashcan. "Forget it."

"I'm just trying to understand." The words were meant for my own ears, but Brae's eyes dart to mine. "Dad's always been the only person she cares about, more than you or me, and now she says 'jump' and I'm supposed to say 'how high?'" The plate I'm racking slams down harder than I intend. "How can she love someone so much that she'd..." *Abandon me.* I growl at my own weakness and have the sudden urge to hit the heavy bag. "...put up with his shit."

"Don't know. I mean...put yourself in her shoes, dude. What would Layla have to do to get you to leave her?"

What the fuck?

He must have read the question in my expression. "Think about it. What if she alienated you from your friends? Would you leave her?"

It takes me all of zero seconds to answer. "No."

He shrugs. "What if she called you names?"

I shake my head.

"Bet you'd leave her if she hit you." He lifts one eyebrow, contradicting his statement.

He knows I'm hopelessly hooked on Layla. There's not much or anything she could do to make me walk away.

"Yeah, yeah, I see what you're saying. But I will say, if Layla wasn't good to our kids, if she..." I have to force the damn words from my lips because even though it's hypothetical, it feels like blasphemy. "If she was emotionally abusing our kids, we'd have issues."

"But would you leave her?"

Damn. The honest truth is...no, I wouldn't leave her. I'd fix her, but never leave.

"Just go home. Hear her out." He rubs his towel over his high-and-tight military haircut. "If it's Layla you're worried about, I'll stay and take care of her until you get home." He winks. *Asshole.*

Even though he's giving me shit, he knows he's one of two guys I'd ever trust keeping an eye on her and Axelle. The other is Jonah, but he's busy with his wife and baby.

"I don't know, man. I mean she's due any day now." What are the chances she'll give birth while I'm gone? Orange County isn't even an hour flight from Las Vegas. I've been at the training center longer than I'd be in Oceanside. I'm running out of excuses not to go.

The door to the weight room swings open and three fighters enter: Wade and two new guys he's been working with.

"Daniels." He greets me, but my brother also turns his head.

"Wade, this is my brother Braeden, United States Marine Corps."

Wade's eyebrows lift. "No shit?" He reaches out a hand, and Brae stands to shake Wade's. "Nice to meet you, and thanks for your service."

Brae cringes slightly, not enough for anyone to notice but me. It irks the shit out of him to take credit for combat he's never actually experienced, but he plays it off well. "Thanks, man. Nice to meet you."

The guys hit the weights, and Brae and I hit the cardio machines in silence. We don't have to talk to know from the dead air between us and lack of teasing jabs our thoughts are on whatever it is waiting for me back in Cali.

And as much as I'd hate to admit it, I'm making flight arrangements in my head.

EIGHT

LAYLA

"As soon as Cameron announces a fight, I open a file here." I click on the program and that opens to multiple files.

I decided after lunch today that the condo was too quiet and I needed something to do, so I came to the training center to go over some last minute things with Eve since she'll be taking over while I'm on maternity leave. "The easiest way to do it—"

"Layla, you've shown me this." Eve's deadpan voice calls my eyes. "Multiple times."

"Oh, well then"—I click off the program—"I can show you how to file the invoices for—"

She groans and drops her head into her hands, fisting her thick blond hair. "You showed me that too." I slump back in my chair, and she swivels hers to face me. "What's going on?"

"Nothing, why would you think something's going on?" I force a light laugh and avoid her piercing glare.

"Why aren't you home? We've been through everything I need to do here. Things are mellow until the next fight, so why not hit maternity leave early?" Her pinched brows and probing blue eyes attempt to read me.

"And do what? Sleep all day?"

"Yes, or any of the other stuff pregnant chicks do like shop for baby shit or eat or do that nesting thing where you reorganize your house."

I've already done all that. And redone it. I push up and arrange papers that don't need arranging. "There're still some things I'm sure we need to go over like..." I run my eyes over the desk, even turn to peek into Cameron's office. "Hm... there's got to be something."

"Layla, stop."

I open my mouth to protest, but learned long ago that arguing with Eve is an auto-lose situation. "Fine."

She blinks down at the floor where my purse is, but quickly brushes off whatever she's thinking. "Look, you're welcome to hang out as long as you want, but you don't have to do it teaching me stuff. We can—" Her gaze darts back to my purse. "You gonna get that?"

"Hm?" I pretend that I don't hear the incessant buzzing of my phone, even though it's been ringing every hour since six a.m. "No, it's probably nothing."

Her eyes pull into tight slits. "How do you know that? It could be important."

The phone continues to buzz. "Nah, Blake's here. He knows where to find me and Axelle's in class."

The buzzing stops, only to start up again.

Eve locks eyes with me, and the phone's vibration suddenly seems like a roar.

"Oh for the love of God." She grabs my purse and fishes out my phone.

I snag the purse back by the strap a little too eagerly, which only tightens her stare.

She hits the screen and puts the phone to her hear. "Hello?"

Shit!

Her eyes widen a little. "Yes, I'm listening."

Oh shit, oh shit, oh shit.

I reach for the phone, but she turns and jumps up from her seat faster than my big ole body can move.

Dammit!

"Yeah, go on."

This is it. Eve's going to find out, tell Blake, and he'll lose his shit and open a whole new world of *what the fuck* right before I have this baby. I can't handle this. I don't want anything to do with any of this.

Her body turns slowly, and her eyes are wide on mine. "I'm going to have to get back to you on that." A few beats of silence. "Okay, bye." She hits End and moves back into her seat, falling back hard and letting her head drop back. "Whoa."

"Eve, listen, I can explain…" But no words come out of my mouth.

Her head lulls to the side. "He says he's Axelle's dad." Her voice is a whisper, and I could hug her for her discretion. Lord knows it's not her usual MO, but the fire of anger keeps my arms locked to my sides.

"I figured."

"Do you remember him?" She's still whispering.

"I don't even know his name. I haven't been answering the calls, and the one time I did I hung up the second I realized he…" I drop my head into my hands and force back the burn of tears. I won't cry over this. I refuse to shed another tear. What's done is done and it brought me my daughter. I can't find it in my heart to regret that.

"His name is Trip Miller."

My breath freezes in my lungs. Trip? My high school crush? The guy I went out of my way to impress, but wouldn't give me the time of day?

"I take it you know him?"

I nod and get lost in my memories. The night I got pregnant with Axelle I went to that party looking for him. I drank and drank, and he never seemed to even notice I was there. He wasn't even friends with Stewart. How did he end up...? Bile rushes into my throat.

I cup my mouth with my hand. "I think I'm going to be sick."

She moves quickly, pulling me to my feet and helping me to the ladies' restroom down the hallway. I race into a stall and vomit everything I'd eaten that day until there's nothing left but spit.

I don't want to do this. "I don't want to face this." Not now.

"I know, Layla, I do, but sooner or later you're going to have to."

I didn't even realize she was so close, but feel the tug of her holding my hair back. I shake my head and wait for another rush of puke that never comes then drop back on my ass, leaning against the adjacent wall.

"This doesn't make any sense. We barely spoke five words to each other." Especially after I ended up a pregnant teenager. He avoided me completely after that bomb dropped. Is this why? "How could he do this to me?" Tears fall in streams down my cheeks as the weight of betrayal sets in.

I was asleep, totally drugged, and he took advantage of me. I thought I loved Trip back then, at that age all love feels like the deepest kind of love. And he treated me like some piece of pass-around pussy.

And now he's claiming to be Axelle's father? What the hell brought that on?

Images of him flash behind my eyes: his deep blue eyes and brown shaggy hair. I remember it was so thick, the kind that women would die to have... just like Axelle's.

A sob rips from my chest.

"That's it. I'm going to get Blake." She moves to leave.

"No!" Panic floods my veins and I try to push myself to standing. "No, please don't."

She gives me her hand and helps me to my feet. "Layla, you can't keep this from him."

"I know, but I need time to figure this out before I talk to him." Between Stewart and now Trip, I don't know what to believe. What do I say? *Hey, Blake. Guess what? We have another guy claiming to be my baby daddy. Maybe in a few years we'll have a baker's dozen.* I groan and rub my temples.

She flushes the toilet, shaking her head. "I don't think that's a good idea."

"Please, Eve." I wipe my eyes and try to pull myself together. "You don't understand Blake. He's protective to a fault. He'll go after Trip and end up back in jail or worse. Just...please." My stomach pinches painfully at my lie. It's not a total lie, but the truth is I don't want Blake to be reminded of my past any more than I do.

Everything we have, everything we've worked to overcome will come crashing down around us. He's already in a weird place with the baby coming and all his responsibilities that go along with it, changing from a single guy to a family of four almost overnight. The information about someone snooping around, which I'm sure now is Trip, is bound to make any man nervous, especially someone as protective as Blake. Yeah, I need to take care of this on my own. Squash it before it reaches him and Axelle.

Fuck, this is all such a nightmare.

My nightmare...the laughing. Was Trip there that night, laughing?

A new wave of hysteria threatens to drop me to my knees, but Eve's eyes are locked on me.

I cough to clear the emotion from my throat. "I think I might head home after all."

She nods, and sympathy shines in her eyes. "Yeah, I think that's smart."

I move to the sink, rinse my mouth out, and clean up my face. "Eve, promise you won't say anything?"

She meets my eyes through the reflection in the mirror. "Yeah, but only if you promise me you'll talk to Blake. You can't handle this on your own. It's too big and you're too fragile right now."

There's pain in her eyes, and I can't help but wonder if she's thinking about what happened with Raven. One minute all was well, and the next Eve was laid up in a hospital bed, praying for her best friend and her baby.

"You don't understand. This has the potential to ruin my life. What if he is Axelle's father? What does that mean for Blake, and how will all this affect him?" A single tear drips down my cheek. "How will it affect us?"

Sympathy softens her eyes and she steps closer. "He has no power. He can't just breeze in, confess he raped you in high school, and waltz away with parental rights."

"You heard how persistent he was with me. What if he tries to contact *her*? Why should she…no, why should we have to pay the price for their cruelty?" A fresh wave of tears pours down my face.

Her eyes widen. "I'm not defending him. I'm not, but…" She chews the inside of her mouth. "What if there's more to the story? He made it sound like whatever it is he wants to tell you is important."

"I can't handle learning more about that night." I sniff back tears and try to compose myself. "I just can't."

Eve's eyes shine as well, and I force myself to turn away, unable to witness her pain on my behalf.

"Eve!" I hear a banging knock on the door and Cameron's bellowing voice. "You in here?"

I sniff and wipe my cheeks. "Crap."

"Yeah, I'm here. Give me a sec."

"You with Layla? Daniels's up here looking for her!" He calls through the door.

"Yeah, I'm here." I take a quick peek at my splotchy face and bloodshot eyes. No way they'll buy that I wasn't crying. Fuck!

Eve lifts her eyebrows, and I nod that I'm as ready as I'll ever be. We move out of the bathroom to find a concerned-looking Cameron. His glare moves between Eve and me, but thankfully his woman wraps her arms around his neck and pulls his lips to hers. "Hey, babe. Just a little girl talk is all."

I duck my chin and move back toward my desk where Blake is sitting, one half of his ass on the top and his hand on his hip. He's wearing training clothes, and his hair looks damp.

"Hey, Bla—"

"What the fuck is going on, Layla?" His eyes move from my forehead to my cheeks, eyes, and land on my lips.

I give him a shy smile and dab my cheeks with my fingertips. "Got a little emotional talking to Eve."

His eyes dart to Eve, who thankfully is still facing Cameron and dropping kisses along his jaw so Blake can't see the guilt she's probably wearing on her expression. "Emotional? Talking about what?"

"Oh ya know…" I roll my eyes. "Babies, puppies, diaper commercials, the normal stuff."

His glare tightens. Shit, he knows I'm lying. I close the space between us, and he opens his legs a little wider to welcome me between them. My arms move to wrap around his neck, and he braces my hips in a firm grip. He opens his mouth to talk, but I beat him to it.

"I was just headed home, wanna come?" I lean in and press a soft kiss on his bottom lip, redirecting him with sex, not my proudest moment.

His eyes flare with desire, and I watch with fascination as the worry that shone in the green depths dissolves a little. "With you, Mouse, I always wanna come."

A genuine giggle bubbles up from my throat, and I'm thankful for the break from all the tears. "Let me grab my stuff and we'll go."

He grabs a handful of my ass and kisses my forehead. "I've got something I need to do, but I'll meet you at home."

"Okay, but"—I run my nose from his shoulder, up his neck, breathing him in, to his ear—"don't shower. Save that for me."

He growls with a hunger so deep that my thighs clench together.

This is where I want to be, where I want to stay. Far away from the memories with a future filled with new memories to make. I refuse to live my life in fear, afraid to turn every corner because there could be some sliver of my past waiting to explode in my face.

But Eve's right. I'm fragile right now, and my number one priority is getting this baby here whole and healthy. Trip waited eighteen years to come forward with whatever information he has about that night. He can wait a little longer. I'll avoid his calls, and he can stay busy digging up records until I'm strong enough to end this once and for all.

Renewed by the little control I've gained in having a plan, I resolve to live in the moment. And as if the universe was out to torture me, my phone starts vibrating again.

Son of a bitch!

NINE

BLAKE

Before I even register the vibration of Layla's phone on her desk, I see her eyes widen a fraction and then relax, trying to cover up her response. She moves to grab it, but I'm closer and snag it before she gets there.

I accept the call. "Who is this?" Not at all in the mood for social niceties, I bark out the question and am met with silence from the end of the line. "Hello?"

"Um…I'm sorry. I'm calling for Ms. Moorehead?" A woman, polite and professional, but fuck hearing that last name is startin' to grate on my nerves. Axelle's legally mine, Layla's carrying my baby and is way the fuck mine, and neither of them have my last name. Yet. "She's here. May I ask who's calling?"

Layla's face has gone pale, and she's sucking on her bottom lip. Is she going to cry?

"Yes, of course. This is Debra Thompson. I'm Axelle's guidance counselor. If this is a bad time, I can call back later."

"Hold on a sec." I hit Mute and reach to pull Layla to me, but she flinches. I hold my hand up and lean away from her. "Mouse, what the hell is going on? You look like you're about to pass out." I grab her desk chair and wheel it to her. "Sit."

With tentative steps, she moves to the chair and drops down. I squat down to eye-level, and she gulps in a quick breath.

"Listen, it's the school. Axelle's fine. It's just her guidance counselor, probably wants to talk about her admission to UNLV."

"Oh my…" She slumps over and leans her forehead into her hand. "I'm sorry. I…I'm not myself lately. I'm sorry."

"Do you want me to have her call you back?"

She nods a few times into her hand.

I hit Unmute and put the phone to my ear while keeping my other hand on Layla's hip. "Mrs. Thompson, if you could call Layla back, we'd appreciate that."

"Sure thing." There's a smile in her voice. "You must be Mr. Daniels?"

"Yes, ma'am."

"Elle speaks highly of you."

"Thank you, it means a lot hearin' that. I always thought teenagers were supposed to hate their parents."

Debra chuckles. "Yes, well…not all of them. I'll try Ms. Moorehead back in a couple hours."

I grit my teeth and nod then say goodbye.

"Hey…" Eve and Cameron step up to us. I almost forgot they were even here. Eve shares a quick moment with Layla; it's that brief non-verbal shit women do with their eyes. "Everything okay?"

"Yeah." Layla takes a shaky breath. "Axelle's guidance counselor called. I just, um…I'm jumpy today."

Not a lot surprises me anymore when it comes to a pregnant woman and her moods, but my guess is her jumpiness has to do with that damn email. I clench my jaw, angry at myself for being so careless. She never should've seen that.

"Right." Eve's eyes bounce between Layla and me, and Cameron seems confused. "Cameron and I are going to head down to the break room and grab a drink." She nods to Layla, more non-verbal crap.

What the hell was that?

I can't help but think something's going on all around me but I'm oblivious to it all. When I look at Cameron, he only scowls and shakes his head. That's non-verbal guy speak for *don't fucking ask me, I'm just as lost as you, brother.*

Whatever it is I brush it off to pregnancy hormones and girl shit and hand Layla her phone. "Debra Thompson is calling you back to talk about Axelle in two hours."

"Great, yeah." She tucks her hair behind her ears. "That's… great. Okay."

I tilt my head, studying her. "You upset about the email?"

"No, no." She shakes her head convincingly. "It's not that. It's just…" She exhales long and hard. "I'm tired, but can't sleep." Her hands brace on our baby. "I'm uncomfortably huge, but can't do anything about it. I'm starving, but can't fit more than a teaspoon of food in my stomach at a time. My joints are all loosey-goosey, my feet are swollen, and I'm just so ready to have this baby and yet completely terrified at the same time." She blinks up at me.

I'm stunned silent, shaking my head.

"What?"

"Fuck!" I rub the back of my neck. "I had no idea."

"Yeah, welcome to my world of crazy." A tiny blush hits her cheeks.

"Brae was going to stop by for dinner tonight, but I'll call him and cancel. I don't want—"

She perks up. "Mmm…are you barbequing?"

"Yeah." I try to hold back my grin.

"Don't cancel." She licks her lips as if she can already taste the food.

Warmth explodes in my chest. Fuck, I love this woman and I hate to see her hurting, and even seeing her uncomfortable is a kick in the nuts. I tug her to me, and she collapses into my chest. "Bossy Mouse."

My conversation with Brae in the weight room comes back to me. This woman is so deep under my skin there's nothing I wouldn't do or sacrifice to keep her, even if it meant my own happiness.

It's nothing like what my mom goes through with my dad, but for the first time, I can see where her devotion to The General comes from.

She loves him so deep down in her soul that torture with him is better than the pain of never having him around. I inhale Layla's hair and feel the shift in my heart where my mother is concerned.

Is it possible she's not as bad as I thought?

—

LAYLA

It's just before sunset and I'm in the kitchen throwing together the finishing touches on a fresh salad while Blake and Braeden entertain Axelle on the patio and grill steaks. It's amazing how much the brothers look alike: same build, dirty blond hair, and those cutting green eyes that Blake says they get from their father, who I've yet to meet.

Blake hasn't talked about him much, but I know his dad is the one who kept him from his gift with music, so I already don't like the guy. But watching their easy laughter and the way they're tuned in to Axelle as she talks about school and her future move to college makes me wonder how bad The General could be to raise two great sons.

I slide the bowl into the fridge and move outside to join the conversation. Before my feet even cross the threshold of the sliding glass doors, Blake's eyes dart to me. I can almost hear his thoughts as he takes in my socked and Ugg-booted feet, leggings, and sweatshirt.

Yes, Blake, I'm warm enough.

His gaze lands on mine and softens before he flashes his signature crooked smile. That look warms me with a different kind of heat, which makes me want to strip naked and fan myself.

He pulls up a chair next to his and nods to it while staying in the conversation with Braeden and Axelle.

"I just can't decide between getting an apartment with some roommates and living in the dorms." Axelle twirls a long strand of her hair.

"Dorms." Blake leans back and takes a long pull off his beer.

"I'm with Blake." Brae nods. "Dorms."

"You'd think that would be the cheaper option, but it's not. I mean"—she shrugs and picks at strings that hang from the hole in the knee of her jeans—"I saw an ad for some people searching for a roommate for only $250 a month. I'd get my own room and—"

"No fuckin' way, Axelle." Blake shakes his head, eyes closed as if he refuses to hear another word.

I open my mouth to reprimand him for his language, but it never helps, so I keep my lips shut.

He rubs his head, irritated. "You're not moving in with people you don't know."

She drops her head back with an exasperated groan. "I don't see what the big deal is."

"Honey, don't get upset." I lean forward and rub her forearm. "He's right. You don't want to shack up with a bunch of strangers. They could be psychos or hoarders or *guys.*"

Blake points to me. "Exactly."

Her eyes widen for a split second before she reins in her reaction. "Ha!" She laughs nervously and then drops her gaze to her lap. "It's not like the dorms will be all that different." She shrugs one shoulder. "I won't know anyone there either."

"Yeah, but dorms have records. And rules. At least you can't get murdered by someone after curfew without it being caught on video surveillance." Brae grins, his smile not as predatory as Blake's. He's more…pretty, less edgy, which somehow makes him seem more dangerous.

"I agree with them, Axelle." I absently rub my baby-ball belly. "How about we compromise? One year on campus, make some good friends, and then you can get an apartment."

"Sounds fair." Blake grabs my hand and gives it a squeeze, peering down at me with pride.

I love him.

"Fine, whatever." She rolls her eyes. "At this point, I'm just hoping I get accepted."

After Axelle's guidance counselor called back, she assured me there's a good chance my daughter will get accepted with her latest test scores, but there's no guarantee. I think she said more, but I had a hard time paying attention with my pulse raging in my ears. Stupid phone rang and I'd shot three inches in the air with a yelp. Blake threw me a curious glare from across the kitchen, clearly noticing my nerviness.

I can't stop thinking about Trip. How in the world did he end up with Stewart and his crew that night? Not that it matters now. Even if he does come forward, there's little I can do legally. The statute of limitations would keep me from trying to prosecute him, so other than a painful admission of guilt, he'd owe no penalty to the state. Chances are he's just a selfish prick looking to free up his conscience.

The sad thing is if he'd given me the time of day back then I would've slept with him willingly. God, this is all so fucking disturbing.

My stomach churns and hunger pangs claw away at my insides, waking the baby. I put my hand on a little hard spot as it rolls across the left side of my belly below my ribcage. "Ah, yeah." I blow out a long breath. "It's getting tight in there, little buddy, I know."

"Is she moving?" Blake leans over and puts both hands on my abdomen. "Hey, baby…" He presses his lips to the rolling part of a human that's jackhammering my lungs. I run my hand through his hair, holding him to me and absorbing the love he's pouring over our baby in whispers.

"I thought you said you didn't know what you were having?" Brae leans forward in his chair, his elbows on his knees, and his eyes fixed on Blake's attention to my tummy.

"We don't. Blake's just convinced it's a girl." I massage my fingers into the back of his neck in soothing circles. "Of course he's wrong. It's totally a boy."

A timid smile pulls at Brae's lips. "Man, that's such a trip. My big brother's gonna be a dad."

Blake peeks up at Axelle. "Already am, bro." A moment of silence descends on us, and my daughter's face goes soft at being claimed by a father.

The past pushes to get in, to remind me of what I have to face sooner or later with regard to Trip and his phone calls, but I refuse to focus on that now.

"Whoa!" Blake pulls his hand back for a split second before placing both hands back on my belly. "Dude, you gotta feel this!"

His eyes are wide, and he motions for Braeden to come over.

Brae kneels at my feet and moves to place both hands on my belly but darts his gaze to mine first. "Layla? May I?"

He's asking permission to touch me? "Of course." I nod and bite my lip against the emotions billowing just below the surface.

The heat of his big hands warms me as he palms my belly like a basketball. His eyes narrow for a second and then close in concentration.

Oh! Huge kick-stretch to the ribs. *Ow.*

"Holy fuck!" His eyes slide to mine. "Damn, little sister, that had to hurt."

I grunt and grit my teeth. "Ah, it's not so bad. Things are getting cramped in there though, so I think he's anxious to get out."

"What was that? A foot?" He moves his hands around to feel again.

"Crazy ass shit, huh?" The light excitement in Blake's voice calls my eyes, and I'm reminded of how lucky I am to have this.

I'm not alone this time.

And if I weren't so lost in my own relief and thoughts of myself, I'd notice the pain radiating from my daughter's eyes.

TEN

BLAKE

Axelle went out with some friends after dinner, and after Layla went to bed, Braeden and I decided to sit on the patio and pop the caps on a couple more beers.

It's been a long time since my brother and I just hung out like this. I missed his adolescent years, only getting to see him on holidays while I was in military school. Not a day goes by that I don't think about what my brother had to deal with after I left. Without The General having me around as a punching bag, I have to believe Braeden took the majority of his wrath.

We never talk about it, but it's pretty obvious our father keeps my little brother on a short leash, which is upsetting. But what's even more of a mind-fuck is why the hell my grown ass brother doesn't tell the man to kiss his ass and take off.

It's as if he lacks the confidence to stand up to the man, which is totally my fault.

Damn, if I could make it up to him, I would.

This'll be a good start or at least a step in the right direction.

"Brae man, can I ask you a question?"

"What's up?"

I keep my gaze focused on the distant mountains. "Do you have plans tomorrow?"

I can see him staring at me from my peripheral vision. "No. Why?"

"You think you can hang with Layla for the day?"

He stares at my profile for a few seconds. "Thank fuck…" He breathes out a long relieved breath. "You're goin'." There's a smile in his voice.

"Yeah, man." I turn toward him. "I'll go, but you have to promise me you'll keep an eye on my woman."

"Got nothing else to do." He shrugs. "Besides, I like my eyes on your woman."

I pin him with a scowl. "I'm serious. Don't fuck around. It's important to me."

The rational side of me knows nothing is going to happen in the six or so hours that I'm gone, but there's no sense in taking chances, not when it comes to her.

"You got it, no fuckin' around." He drops his head back to stare up at the sky. "Tomorrow. That'll be perfect."

I glare at him. "Perfect for what?"

"It's Saturday. Dad'll be home." He says it as if it's no big thing, as if Dad and I'll spend the afternoon watching a game and fighting over whose team is better.

"And that's good?"

His expression grows serious. "It is."

"I don't get any of this, but I swear to shit if I end up getting ambushed by some parental dilemma I will hunt you down and beat the snot out of you."

I expect a smile, maybe even a laugh, but all he does is dip his chin in understanding.

"Not gonna lie, man. This is the weirdest crap you've ever asked me to do."

"It'll make sense soon enough, brother." He pushes up and takes another pull off his beer. "I'm off."

A small grin tilts my lips. "Oh so that's it? You got what you want, so you're out?" I mock pout. "I feel so used."

"Don't act like you care." He moves through the open door and into the kitchen. The sound of his empty bottle hitting the trash can filters out from inside. "It's been fun, but I've got a date with a manipulative Vegas girl." He throws the words over his shoulder as he passes through the living room.

I don't walk him out, but stay with my ass planted on my patio. "Use a rubber!"

"Idiot," he mumbles just before I hear the front door open and close.

Shit…I'm going back to Orange County tomorrow. I didn't tell my brother that I already booked my flight, just in case I changed my mind.

But it's done now. I just hope I don't regret it.

After I suck down the last of my beer, I head to bed and find Layla sitting up, her back against the headboard, glasses on, and remote pointed at the television.

Click. Click. Click.

I move through the room, taking off my clothes and throwing on some flannel pants. The TV screen continues to flash with different channels, her eyes glazed over and staring.

Click. Click. Click.

I stand at the edge of my side of the bed, moving my gaze back and forth between my zoned-out woman and the flicking television screen.

"Mouse, baby, you going for a record?"

"Huh?" Her eyes move to me, and she pushes up her glasses at the bridge of her nose.

I point to the remote. "There. You trying to see how many clicks you can get in a solid hour? Going for Guinness book?"

A tiny blush colors her cheeks. "Oh"—she drops the remote onto the down comforter—"no, I was just looking for something to watch."

"Right." I pull back the sheet and crawl in next to her, pulling her down and onto my chest. "Maybe you could hold off for a second? I need to talk to you about something."

She tilts her face up, resting her chin on my chest, worry pinching her brows. "Sure, what's up?"

"Turns out my presence has been *requested* in Orange County." I run my knuckles up her soft cheek and pull her glasses off to place them on my bedside table.

She blinks rapidly before her eyes widen. "The General?"

"No, if it were him who wanted me there, he'd just show up and drag me back or send his thugs to get me." A humorless laugh burst from my lips and sadness washes over her face. I run my thumb between her eyebrows to smooth the worry. "Actually, it's my mom. Guess she gave up trying to get me to come home, so she sent Brae."

"That's great, right?" The corner of her mouth lifts a little. "You miss her; you have to."

I shake my head and sift my fingers through her hair. At first I didn't know why Layla twirled her hair so much, but now I get it. The shit's as soft as anything I've ever felt. "I don't know how I feel. Not sure what she's planning on dropping on me, but I'm not exactly pissin' myself with excitement to find out."

Her eyes dart to the side, and then she turns her head to rest her cheek back on my chest. "Crap. I mean I think it's a really good idea to go, but I can't travel so close to my due date."

"Not you, babe, they're requesting me and me alone."

Her stunned gaze swings back to mine, and I can't help but groan against the disappointment I see.

"Don't take it personally. It's only a day trip, and it could get ugly. I wouldn't want you there for that anyway." I continue to run my fingers through her hair and down to massage her neck. "Think of it like this. Maybe if I can work things out with them and if they agree to be on their best behavior, I'll see if they want to come down for a few days after the baby comes."

"Okay." She seems to relax a little, but I can still feel the slight tensing of her muscles. "I'd like that. I mean...the more family the better. My parents don't travel well, and I wouldn't feel comfortable having them too far from the nursing home."

"We'll take the baby to visit them in Florida as soon as we get the okay to do so." I speak the words into the top of her head between kisses.

"Thank you." She sighs softly into my chest, and the breathy sound has me hardening instantly.

Sooner I get this conversation over, the sooner I can get inside my woman. "So tomorrow I'm going to have Brae spend the day with you while I take a quick trip back home."

Her body tenses. "I don't need a babysitter."

"I know."

"Then why have Braeden come?"

"Because I'll be dealing with enough in Orange County, and knowing he's here with you'll buy me a little peace of mind."

"Blake—"

"Please, Mouse. It's for a day. I'll be back by dinner."

She huffs out a breath that sounds a lot like the one Axelle did earlier when we threw down the dorm rule. "Fine."

I press my lips to the top of her head and whisper there. "Thank you."

"What time do you leave?"

I flex my hips and roll her over, settling myself to her side, but sliding my thigh up along hers to lock her in place. "Flight leaves at nine a.m." My fingers dance up her bare arm with a light touch that raises goose bumps against her flesh. "Which means it's time for you to get naked."

She squirms as much as she can with my leg thrown over hers, her eyelids drooping with every barely there touch against her skin. A low moan falls from her lips before she bites the bottom one and arches her back. I trace the delicate line of her jaw and run my thumb along her lower lip to free it from her teeth. Her legs continue to press against mine, as if she's trying to put out a fire or open them for me.

Burying myself inside Layla is the only therapy I need before I face whatever's going on back home. And that's exactly what I plan to do.

ELEVEN

BLAKE

My fingertips tingle as I glide them along every bit of Layla's exposed skin. It's as if every part of her is an erogenous zone when we're together. No matter where I touch, she responds immediately.

I dip my head, running my lips along her shoulder, allowing my tongue to dart out as I follow the line of her collarbone with my forefinger. "Damn, Mouse. You smell and taste so fucking good."

She tries to push me over, get me on my back, and have her wicked way with me, but she's not the one in control tonight. I need this more than I need air, need to feel her warmth wrapped around me before I return to face my past. I hope that she can send me off with enough of that warmth to beat back the old demons that'll threaten to get inside.

"Blake…" Her words dissolve with a shaky plea that I'm all too familiar with.

I don't plan on making her suffer, but first…"Mouse?" I speak the name against her skin, allowing my tongue another taste of her sweet neck.

"Mmm?" Her hands grip my hair, holding me to her.

"I wanna fuck you in The Room."

Her breath hitches, and her body melts deeper into the bed as if my words have just turned her into pure liquid.

I smile against her pulse point. "Can I assume that's a yes?"

"Yes, please."

I can't help the tiny chuckle that bubbles up from my throat and hits her neck in a hot burst. "So polite, my Mouse." I continue to bathe her chest and neck in soft kisses, my hand moving to the hardened pink tips of her breasts, which I can see through her thin tank top. "I wanna hear you ask me, baby. I want to know that you want that bad enough you'd ask me for it."

Her body freezes, and I pull back to see the flare of rebellion in her eyes. I run my thumb over her nipple in long but firm passes until a haze of desire washes away the urge to fight me.

"I want you to take me to your music room." She forks her fingers into my hair, scraping her nails along my scalp the way she knows I like it.

I groan and my hips jerk forward, rubbing myself against her thigh. "Say please." Fuck, she's got me so worked up my voice sounds weak in my own ears.

Her hand slides down and grips my hard-on. "You first."

"Dammit, woman." I push up and do a quick rearrangement of my pants for comfort then scoop a satisfied-looking Layla off the bed. "You're learning all my tricks, beating me at my own game."

She giggles and buries her head into my neck. "So punish me."

"Fuckin' hell, now she's asking to be punished, as if I wasn't already about to explode." I growl and move out of our room and down the hallway to the one room in the house that has always been locked...until Layla. I kick the door open, flick on the lights, and bring her to the worn leather couch.

The smell of maple, birch, and mahogany soothes my nerves, and the view of my woman, flushed with arousal and need, stirs my blood. I shut and lock the door then turn toward her. She leans back on the couch, her tiny shorts and tank top showing off a healthy portion of her swollen belly.

I move to stand at her feet and glare down at her. "Up."

"Up?" She scopes the area, almost as if she's wondering where else there is to make love if we're not doing it on the couch.

I nod and offer her my hand, knowing that it's not easy for her to push herself to standing. Once she's up, I turn her around, gripping her hips firmly until she presses her ass against my dick.

Yeah, now she gets it. There are only a few positions that are comfortable for her at this stage in pregnancy, and luckily they're all my favorite ones. Then again, every position with Layla is a favorite.

My hands run from her hips around to her belly. I rest my chin on her neck, and she tilts her head, inviting my lips. There's a small strand of hair in the way, so I blow gently to gain access to her sweet skin. She shivers in my arms and my dick jumps.

After I spend a short time on her neck, her ass rubbing against me, her hands dip beneath my pants and she digs her fingernails into my ass. Need rides me hard, and I tug at the tender flesh of her neck with my teeth.

I suck deep and hard at her neck as if I could ingest her goodness and love. Like a starving man, I gorge myself and *know* that nothing the world can offer will ever satisfy me as she does.

Moving down her body, I drop to my knees behind her, pulling her shorts down to her ankles. I don't have to ask; she freely steps out of them and I toss them aside.

At eye level with her ass, I groan at how fucking perfect she looks. The curve of her hips and round globes of her cheeks are fuller now, and my teeth tingle to sink into the soft flesh. Might have to keep her pregnant all the time.

I lick my lips before placing a kiss on her backside. She drops her head forward; her hands cover mine, which are on her hips.

"Knees on the couch." My command is low and throaty, and she shivers in response as she does what I ask.

Kneeling on the couch, she leans forward to place her elbows on the back. The visual is almost too much to take, and I stare for several seconds to commit the view to memory.

"Hell, Mouse…never seen anything so beautiful in my whole life."

She ducks her chin, and I know this must be hard for her. She's mentioned how self-conscious she is with all the changes her body is going through. If only she could see herself through my eyes.

I run my hands up the front of her thighs and around to her ass, preparing her for my attention. "Arch your back, baby."

She does, giving me all the invitation I need. I dip down and kiss her between her legs. Long and deep, I use my tongue to blaze a trail that I plan to soon follow with my dick.

She walks her knees wider and presses back into my lips. Every lap of my tongue, nip of my teeth, and slide of my mouth has her moaning and moving against me. Words fall from her lips in jumbled strings, and if I weren't so lost in her taste, I might've grinned.

"Don't stop…" Her hips roll as she works herself against my face.

Aw, fuck, my stomach tightens with the building orgasm that is sure to end all orgasms.

I pull back and she whimpers loud.

"Shhh, baby." I stand and align myself with her. "I've got you."

"Blake, hurry." She leans her forehead on the back of the couch, pushing herself out to me.

Slowly, I nudge my way in, and my jaw falls loose at the overwhelming feeling, the awe-inspiring sight, and the sensory overload that is sliding inside Layla. No matter how many times I do it, it never ceases to rock me to the core. Her tiny body, so in tune with mine, nothing has ever felt like a coming together of mind, body, and soul like making love to her.

With intentional strokes, I glide in and out, absorbing the warmth of her delicate body. I bite my lip, and my legs tense to hold back and remain gentle while everything in me begs to power into her. To lose myself completely and claim her with an aggression that she'll feel for days.

Her breathing gets heavy, puffs of air from her lips mixed with the tender whispers of my name. My chest swells with pride, love, and devotion to her, us, our family. Our future.

She rocks back into me, asking for more, letting me know that she can take it. I quicken my pace, but lock down the urge to go deeper. She moans and I know she's close. I rock into her again and again then lean forward and kiss her shoulder once before pulling at her skin with my teeth.

Her head flies back in a flurry of blond hair, and she groans my name through open lips. With her head turned slightly, I push up and claim her mouth. Her tongue pushes past my teeth, and I suck it deep into my mouth, hoping she can taste herself. Leveraging against the couch, she rocks back into me.

I grin, small and quick, before pulling back and stilling her hips with my hands. "Easy."

She drops her head heavy and stills to allow me to control the speed and depth. Starting slowly, I pull almost all the way out and then glide back in. She moans. I do it again, a little faster, and pick up the speed with every thrust.

"Don't stop…" Her muscles tense and thrust forward through the gripping pressure, knowing she's close.

She reaches back with one hand, and her nails dig into the flesh of my hips, spurring me on. I lean over, resting my hand on hers that grips the back of the couch, holding her in place as I roll my hips with a final thrust that tips her over the edge. She pants through the orgasm that shreds through her body while I hold her firmly to me.

I drop kisses along her shoulder until I feel her body relaxing. "You good, baby?"

"Mmmm…" Damn if there isn't a smile in her moan.

I push up and start to move, satisfied that my woman is ready for more. With a tightening in my gut, I throw more weight behind my hips, again and again, then nuzzle my forehead into her back. I want to shout how much I love her, write her fucking poetry, and quote romantic sonnets, but instead I bite against the roar of my own release. My eyes pinch closed as the intensity washes over me, making me dizzy for a second before the feeling in my legs comes back.

"You okay?" I kiss her shoulder and move my hand from her hip to wrap around our baby in her belly. "If anything's going to throw you into labor"—I pant, catching my breath—"it's that orgasm." I roll my forehead against her shoulder. "Damn, thought that thing would kill me."

She giggles, soft but throaty, and the sound alone has me hardening again. "You always say that."

"What?" I push up and massage her lower back. "I do not."

She pushes up and leans back into my chest, keeping our connection. "Yeah…you do."

"Well shit, Mouse, surprised I'm not dead by now." I pull away and dip down to grab her panties and shorts. "Wanna clean up before you put these back on?"

"No, I'll put them on just in case Axelle's home. Good thing this room is sound proof." Her eyes widen. "Can you imagine if I ran out of here naked from the waist down and she had friends with her out there?" Her hand covers her mouth and she laughs.

"She'll be away at college before you know it, and then you can do all the streaking through the house that your little heart desires." I tuck myself back inside my sleeping pants then drop to my knees. Layla puts a hand on my shoulder to steady herself while I help her into her panties and shorts.

I glance up and see our baby growing in her belly. My hands move to her on instinct, drawn to the child that any day now I'll hold in my arms. I put my lips to Layla's belly. "Hey, baby, listen…I have to leave town for a few hours tomorrow. You be good and don't give your mama or Uncle Brae a hard time, okay?" I press my ear to her belly. "You'll be good for Mom, but not your Uncle, huh?" I shrug and move my lips against her skin. "Good enough, but um…one more thing." My throat gets tight as if I'm carrying a ten-pound weight inside it. "I love you. I'll always love you. I'll be the first and the last man who'll love you 'til his dying breath. You hear that, baby? First and the last."

Layla's breath hitches in her throat, and I take the moment to close my eyes and settle into the feeling. Love. Unconditional love in all its fucking glory and all around me.

With that, I can face insurmountable obstacles, and a half-day visit with my parents tops that list.

TWELVE

BLAKE

It's eight fifteen a.m. when we pull up to the airport. I thought I'd be up all night with worry, but with our making love in The Room combined with Layla's warm body pressed against mine, I slept like the dead.

Even now, as I hop out of the Rubicon at the terminal curbside, I feel pretty good about seeing my folks. I still don't know what the hell's going on, but my gut tells me it's some form of fence mending that'll give them access to their first grandchild.

Braeden passes me and stops short as he rounds the hood to take the driver's seat. "I'm taking care of your girl." He holds up a set of car keys. "You take care of mine." He lifts an eyebrow over his Maverick-wanna-be sunglasses. "Do you remember where she is?"

I snag his keys and shove them in my pocket. "Long-term parking, spot J-32."

"Yes, and I swear to God if you so much as rip one in my car I'll know"—he rakes his sunglasses up on his head, eyes narrowed—"and I will hunt you down."

"Idiot." I shove past him and roll my eyes at his answering chuckle.

Since the Jeep is lifted, I asked Layla to stay in and told her I'd come around to say goodbye. I open the passenger-side door, and she's pressing buttons on her phone, texting maybe.

She shoves her phone into her purse and smiles a little bigger than I appreciate.

"Shit, baby, don't look so broken up over my leaving." I pull her into my arms for a long hug, and she wraps hers around me as best she can at the awkward angle.

"You said you'd be home by dinner." She pulls back and rests her forehead against mine. "What did you expect? Tears?"

I kiss the tip of her nose. "You cry during cat litter commercials, Mouse. So yeah, I fuckin' expected tears."

She shakes her head, our foreheads still touching. "If you chase around a feather at the end of a stick, then I'll see what I can do for you."

Brae climbs into the driver's seat. "Don't worry, bro. I'll take good care of your woman." His eyebrows pinch together in concentration. "Let me see if I remember your instructions." He pinches the bridge of his nose. "Oh, okay, yeah…lots of Vikings reruns, cuddles, and a sponge bath. In that order." He winks.

I glare at him, but my lips curl into a smile. "Right, and I'll make sure to wash your car with a baseball bat and battery acid before I leave."

"Hm, oil massages are great for pregnant women I hear, and something about kegels, which I'm excited to learn more about."

I burst into laughter, wondering if my brother did an Internet search on pregnancy to stockpile ammo to use against me. "I'm thinking I might need to do a little four-wheeling in a rock garden before I come home."

"Boys, boys, no fighting around the pregnant lady. Laughing makes me pee."

Brae's eyes dart to her. "Eww."

I shake my head. "Dude, pee is the least of the *ewws* when it comes to pregnancy."

She smacks my arm, grinning. "Oh you love all my *ewws*. Now go; you have a plane to catch."

"I love *eww*."

She snorts with laughter, leans in, and presses her sweet lips to mine. "Go and hurry home."

After a few more kisses and some pushing from Braeden for me to get my tongue outta my girl and get on the damn plane, I say goodbye and head off to board a flight that is taking me to who knows what back in Oceanside.

—

LAYLA

I wave goodbye to Blake through the Rubicon's window. He stays with his eyes on the vehicle until we're out of sight. My heart dips at watching him disappear and leaving him to face The General on his own.

"So what's on the agenda today, boss?" Braeden turns and peeks at me from the corner of his eye, probably terrified to take his focus off the road after the slew of threats Blake tossed out.

"Hmm…it's Saturday, so you can start with the laundry then the bathrooms. The toilets could use a good scrubbing. All the grout in the tile needs to be done with bleach and a toothbrush." I turn my gaze out my side window to hide my smile.

"Damn, and here I thought I left the military base." I turn just in time to see him salute me. "Ma'am, yes, ma'am!"

I salute back. "At ease, soldier."

A comfortable silence stretches between us, and I fumble with my purse strap. "Ya know you don't have to stay with me all day." I grit my teeth, waiting for his lecture on the sanctity of a promise.

"Yeah, I know my brother's being a little overprotective. We'll play it by ear, okay? I need to be close just in case something happens, but I think as long as you check in and let me know you're okay, I suppose I could let you shower alone."

I swat his arm. "Ha, ha. Guess it's back to cleaning then, Braeden-ella."

"Fuck, where's a fairy godmother when a guy needs one."

"I believe there's—" The shock of my phone's vibration at my hip cuts off my clever quip.

Crap! Maybe pretending I don't feel it is best. I told myself the next Unavailable call that comes in I'm going to answer, but I can't in front of Braeden.

"You should get that." He motions to my purse. "It could be Blake."

Shit, shit, shit!

"Oh…yeah." Ugh. I dig for my phone, pretending I can't find it and hoping it'll stop ringing before I do. It does, and I check the screen to make sure it wasn't Blake.

Unavailable.

The single word sets my pulse rocketing through my veins.

This is the second time he's called this morning. He doesn't leave a voicemail, and I try to calm my nerves.

"Not Blake then?"

"No, just a friend from work. I'll call her later." My cheeks flame at my lie.

That never would've worked with anyone else. Everyone knows there are very few women who are employed by the UFL, and I would never be friends with the ones who are, with the exception of Eve.

"This is a great song." I turn up "No Use for a Name," not even paying attention to the song, just looking for the distraction. Music fills the space for the rest of the ride home while my phone continues to vibrate in my hand.

Enough is enough. This has to stop.

It's time to face the past head on.

———

By the time we pull up to the condo, my phone has rung four different times, and now I'm getting the short buzzes that indicate text messages. Is he texting now too?

I don't dare read them and vow to wait until I'm home behind a locked door before I steel my emotions to Trip's attempts at contacting me. We park in Blake's designated spot, and I see the Bronco is gone. Axelle must be out with a friend. I'll have the condo to myself, except...

"Hey, Brae? Could you do me a favor?" I say before I'm out of the truck.

"Sure." He turns his shoulders toward me, really listening and aiming to please.

"I'm having this intense craving for Rice Krispie treats, but I don't have the stuff to make them."

"You want me to hit the store and grab the shit you need to make 'em?"

"If you don't mind." *And even if you do, yes please.*

"You gonna make some for me too?" He gazes down at me through slits in his eyes.

"Fine, you can have one." I force a smile, but my phone buzzes again and I need to handle this situation before my bravery wears off. I press my hand to my lower belly. "Oh, boy. I gotta pee bad!"

"Whoa..." He recoils. "TMI. Tell me what you need and skedaddle before you soil Blake's leather seats."

"Rice Krispies, marshmallows, and butter!" I wave and hop down from the Rubicon, dancing for a minute just for show before I race off as fast as my Weeble Wobbles body will carry me.

I hear the engine fire up and pull away, so I grab my phone while walking. Five new text messages?

Picking up my pace, I scurry inside the house, hurry to my bedroom, and shut and lock the door.

First, I scroll through Unavailable's messages.

Layla, please pick up the phone. I just want to talk to you.
Then the next.
It'll only take a minute, I swear.
And the next.
I understand why you don't want to talk to me,
but you don't know the whole story.
And again…
If you'd just give me a chance to explain.
And finally.
Please answer.

My phone vibrates, and I answer it before the caller ID even shows up. Not that it matters. I know who it is. "Hello?"

"Oh…uh, Layla?"

"What do you want, Trip?"

A beat of silence. "Look, I know when we last spoke…"

He's remembering his conversation with Eve, but I don't correct him.

"…was a shock to you and I'd hoped you would've remembered."

"I remember nothing. *Nothing* because I was drugged the night I was gang raped and ended up pregnant with a baby no one would fucking claim, Trip! So no, I don't fucking remember anything." Acid churns in my stomach, and my head gets light with the anger of eighteen years.

"Shit, Layla…I…I didn't know—"

"You didn't know? That's fucking laughable! How could you not know? Here's a clue, Trip, and please for the safety of women everywhere, do try to keep up. When a woman is *incoherent*, she's incapable of giving consent!"

"God, I can't even imagine what you must think of me."

The plastic case on my phone protests under my unyielding grip. "Oh, dig deep into the depths of hell, Trip. I'm sure you'll come up with something close."

"It didn't happen the way you think it did. That's what I'm trying to tell you, Layla."

What? What's he saying? "Didn't happen the way…" I shake my head. "No, I don't have time for this. I don't…" I can't consider that things didn't happen exactly the way Stewart described, but then again, when has Stew ever *not* lied?

"You told me you loved me." His whisper is so faint I almost wonder if he didn't mean for me to hear him.

I told him I loved him? But how? I was gone. Passed out cold.

"Let me tell you my version of the story." The pleading sound of his voice perks my ears, but my stomach is heavy with dread.

"I'm afraid of any other version, Trip."

"I understand, but…if you'd give me an hour, just one hour, I could come to Vegas and—"

"Why are you doing this? I don't want to relive this. I…I'm sorry, I have to go."

"Please, don't hang—"

I hit End and send a quick text to Blake, who won't get it until he's off the plane.

If you need me, call Braeden's phone. Love you. xL

I power down my phone and shove it to the bottom of my sock drawer. Out of sight, out of mind.

Well, at least out of sight.

THIRTEEN

BLAKE

It's almost noon when I pull my brother's charcoal-gray Mustang GT into the driveway of my parents' house. The Mexican-style architecture of the old house doesn't make me think of family holidays or summers spent skateboarding in the street. It all brings me back to the night I was taken to military school.

I've been back to visit a half dozen times since I left the Corps, but no matter how many times I come back, the driveway holds a memory I can't seem to shake.

I throw the car in park and push up and out, my feet hitting the pavement almost on the exact spot where I broke my dad's nose. It's been years, and I still search for the bloodstain that faded a long time ago.

With a deep breath of the briny ocean air, I square my shoulders and push back the nervousness that started building the second my plane flew out of Las Vegas airspace. It's as if the further away I got from Layla, from my home, the more my anxiety built.

My hand absently pats my phone in my pocket, reminding me that Layla is a phone call away. It's only a few hours before I have to head back to the airport. Surely I can endure anything for a few hours.

I ring the bell and shove both hands in my pockets.

A few clicks of the locks and the door swings open so quickly that a small gust blows the loose strands of my mom's light brown hair. "Blake." Her eyes are wide and her lips parted, as if she's breathing through the emotion to avoid letting it overtake her.

Not showing emotion. No hugs. Nice to see nothing has changed.

"Hey, Mom." I take in her jeans and pale green collared shirt. Even when I was a kid, she only wore jeans on the weekends. I never thought about it much, but now I have to wonder if that was her choice or The General's demand.

"Come in." She steps back to allow me inside, and it's as if I'm stepping back in time. Everything looks the same from the pale yellow wall color to the antique furniture. Even the lulling tick of the grandfather clock that my dad brought home from a garage sale still sounds through the otherwise silent house.

I move past my mom to the living room with the hope that she'll make this quick so I can get back to my life in Vegas. "I don't have a lot of time. My plane leaves at five."

She pushes back a wisp of hair that's fallen down from where the rest is wrapped at the back of her head. "Oh, so soon?"

I sit on the couch, and she takes one of the chairs across from me.

"Yeah, Mom, Layla's about to have a baby. I need to stay close. I'm sure you can understand that." Fuck, I can already feel the burn of anger stir in my chest and the sound of my father's voice in my own.

"Of course." She drops her chin and fumbles with a kitchen towel she has wadded in her hands. "I'd love to meet her someday."

Good, at least we're getting right to the point.

"I'd like that too, Mom, but Layla's had it rough. When Dad and I get in the same room together, shit goes south quickly. Layla and Axelle can't be around that. I won't allow it."

"Axelle is your adopted daughter, right?"

"Layla's daughter, and yes, now my daughter too." Just saying their names makes my chest feel warm.

She shifts in her chair keeping her back straight and her knees together, the picture of pristine discomfort. "Braeden says Axelle is very smart."

"She is. And she's strong, just like her mom." *And nothing like you.* My jaw aches as I bite down hard against blurting something hurtful.

"And you," she whispers.

"What?"

She lifts her gaze to meet mine. "She's strong like you."

I shrug, not comfortable taking any kind of compliment from my mom.

"Are you still playing?" She doesn't whisper as if it's a dirty little secret as she used to, but her eyes dart toward the bedrooms out of habit.

"Every day. I've even been working with Axelle, teaching her the basics. She's picking up the guitar like a champ." I shouldn't be angry anymore, but every word fires from my lips like a bullet aimed straight for her heart. I want her to know that I'm encouraging my kid toward music rather than treating her interest in it like a fucking disease.

She dips her forehead and nods. "That's great."

Shame twists in my gut, and the impulse to get on with it is overwhelming. "So you sent Brae to get me to come home. You got me here, now what?"

Her eyes slide to the hallway that leads to three bedrooms, including hers, before she turns back to me. "Would you like something to drink? Or eat?" She stands. "I could make you a sandwich."

I glare at her and want to yell for her to just get it over with already. "Make me a…Mom? Just tell me why you want me here. What was so important that you had to send Brae?"

She sits back down and takes a deep breath. The air between us is thick with her silence, and I start to wonder if she even heard me.

"Mom, spit it—"

"Diane?" The General's deep voice echoes from the hallway that leads to their bedroom. "We have company?"

Her eyes widen, and she tilts her head toward his voice, but keeps her eyes on me. "Yes, honey. Blake's here."

The only sound coming from the hallway is shuffling, and out of habit, I stand to greet my father. He comes around the corner, and all the air leaves my lungs in a whoosh.

"Dad…" It's not what I call him, and even as the single word left my lips, I wondered why it came as easily as it did. I clear my throat. "Sir?"

"Son." His steely green stare fixes on mine for a second before he drops his gaze and continues to move toward my mom and me. He's smaller than he was the last time I saw him, his usual military posture now that of an old man. His hair seems to have grayed even more, and what used to be strikingly sharp facial features now seem gaunt. But even still, his presence fills the room.

My mom moves to help him to the chair she was sitting in, but he waves her off and drops into the one right next to it, allowing his wife to keep her spot.

Once seated, he takes a breath as if just trudging across the room cost him all his energy. "I see your brother was more persuasive than I gave him credit for."

His voice calls me back to the present, and I sit back down, elbows on my knees, ass on the edge of the couch. "What's going on, sir? You look…" I can't even put a name on what he looks like.

The corner of his mouth twitches. "Look like shit?"

I nod and shrug one shoulder. "I mean, yeah. Last time I saw you, when you came to Vegas, you seemed fine."

His expression twists in a grimace. "About that, Blake…" He sets his eyes on me, and now that I get a closer look, those too look pale. "I didn't give you the benefit of the doubt. I assumed you were causing trouble when you weren't, and I'm…" He licks his lips, preparing for something that is so foreign it's probably painful. "I'm sorry. I wish I could take back the things I said."

His apology knocks me back with a jerk. I blink, stutter, and search for a proper response. I'm shocked by his apology, but it doesn't take away the sting that years of his rejection have caused. "It's, um…nice of you to say that, but what's done is done. I could've used your support back then when I was locked up. Some things are too old to take back."

He pins me with a thoughtful stare, not intimidation as much as introspection. "I hope that's not true."

I gaze at my mom, who has tears in her eyes, and what started as anxiety flares into widespread fucking fury. Even now, I can't help but feel as if they're fucking with me. Jerking me around without letting me in on the why of this mindfuck.

"Tell me what the hell is going on, or I swear to Christ I'll walk out of here and never come back." My breathing speeds up, and I can't hold back the waterfall of anger that's threatening to spill.

My dad holds up a shaky hand. "Calm down—"

"Don't you fucking tell me to calm down! You haven't spoken to me but to tell me how disappointed you are in me and tell me what a fuck up I am, and now that I'm here, you look like you're knockin' on death's door and apologizing? I left my family, my very pregnant fiancée, to be here, so do me the courtesy of filling me in so I can get the fuck gone." I run two hands over my scalp, begging to keep it together. "Just stop messing with my head."

"Duke." Mom's call of my dad's name sounds almost frantic, as if he has the power to make things right, and she's pleading with him to do so.

He lifts his chin in a show of stoicism. "I'm dying."

And the world fucking stops. Life hits pause. The room, our expressions, everything except the steady thud of my heart.

Thump, thump. Thump, thump. Thump, thump.

"What did you say?" I whisper, but my voice sounds distant, as if I'm calling from another room.

"I have stage-four pancreatic cancer." He's sitting up tall, acting as if he's just told me the headline of today's news.

My thumping heart drops into my gut. "You're undergoing treatment?"

"There's treatment that could buy me some time, but there's no cure."

"What treatment?" That must explain why he looks so beaten up, as if he's been put through the ringer and laid out wet.

"Your dad is refusing treatment, Blake. He's choosing against it because the odds are—"

"Whoa. What?" The question is spit from between my clenched teeth. Am I hearing what I think I'm hearing? He's dying without a fight?

He clears his throat. "The treatment available to me is chemo and radiation. I don't want to live out the rest of my days sick all the time."

I throw a hand out in his direction. "What do you call this? You're sick now!"

He nods, unable to argue with the truth. "I don't feel that bad. Just tired."

"Are you fucking kidding me?" The anger behind my words fuels my body, and I push to stand then pace. "So that's it? No one else gets a say. You're choosing to die?"

Why the hell do I care? This guy hasn't given a shit about me my entire life, and now he's dying and still proving he doesn't give a shit. Fathers who care fight for their lives, if not for themselves, for their kids, for their grandkids.

I grip the sides of my head to avoid putting my fist through a wall. Braeden knew. This is why he insisted I come home, why he wanted me to see The General. Fuck, I have no explanation as to why this news feels like an A-bomb to the gut, but it does.

"It's *my* life and I'm given a choice on how I want it to end." Even though he's sick and clearly weak, his voice still carries an authority that demands attention. "This is it, and honestly, I'm surprised you care as much as you do."

He's not the only one.

He took everything away from me: my music, the trust I had in my mom. He belittled me and locked me up in military school to make sure I stayed away from the thing I loved most in the world. He did that. He never believed in me, never gave me permission or the freedom to follow my dreams and cast my own future. I was ashamed of my music my entire life until Layla. That's all because of him. So yeah, why the fuck does it feel as if I'm swallowing a golf ball and my eyes are burning?

The room feels too small. I need to get the fuck out of here.

Without another word, I move to the door, throwing it open so hard I'm sure it left a dent. I avoid the car out of fear that driving might be the end of me. *Some of us* make staying alive for our kids a priority.

As soon as my feet hit the sidewalk, I look left, then right, and take off running.

FOURTEEN

LAYLA

After Braeden got back from the store with Rice Krispie treat ingredients, I insisted I needed a trip to Baby Mart to shop in an effort to get out of the house. Knowing that my phone is stashed in my sock drawer is too much of a temptation because that conversation with Trip has me more curious than I'd like to admit.

He made the night I got pregnant with Axelle sound like something completely different. I don't know Trip at all. After that night at the party, he basically ignored me, and I was too caught up in the stress of becoming a teenage mother to give a shit about him. A few months into our senior year he disappeared. Rumors around school said he went to juvie, others that his parents shipped him across the country to live with an aunt. Either way, my days of crushing on Trip were over the morning I woke up naked in the back of Stewart's 4-Runner.

I mindlessly flip through newborn onesies while lost in my thoughts.

Did I really tell him I loved him? My face heats with a fire so intense that I already know the answer to that. I'm sure I did.

Enough of this! I'm shopping to keep my mind off this crap, not to dwell on it.

I move to the next aisle and find Brae studying the silicone cups of a breast pump on display. He turns it in his hand, sticks one cup to his eye, and then the other. What is he doing? I cover my mouth to avoid him hearing me giggle as he presses the cups to his swollen pecs.

In his black cargo pants and long-sleeved gray thermal, he looks all military badass and gets the attention of a few women nearby. He has no idea he's gained an audience as he flips the cups around in his hands one more time before facing them out, holding them like guns. He makes realistic explosion noises with his mouth while fake-firing the breast pump cups at random items throughout the store. An unflattering, guttural giggle bursts from my lips.

He turns toward me, a half smile pulling at his mouth. "You think this works?" He presses the cups back to his pecs, his eyebrows dropped low in genuine curiosity.

I roll my eyes and head toward him, laughing. "Why, you thinking of getting one?"

"I don't know." He studies it some more. "Looks kinky to me."

I rest my hand on a hip, cock my head, and glare. "I bet a soccer ball would look kinky to you."

He closes his eyes, bites his lip, and moans so deep a few of the women watching lean in toward him. "God, Layla…" He groans. "Don't mention soccer balls when we're in public. They get me so hot." He lowers one cup to his crotch, but I rip it from his hand before he's able to follow through. "Hey, I was playing with that," he says with a childlike pout.

I swear I hear a woman swoon. I swat his bicep and shove him to move on down the aisle. "You're disgusting."

We pass by his all-female audience, and Brae flashes them his most panty-melting smile. "Any of you ladies want to point me to the nearest sporting goods store?"

I throw my head back laughing and speed walk ahead of him to avoid the embarrassing reactions that I'm sure he's getting.

He catches up with me, chuckling, when his phone rings. He pulls it from his pocket, and his eyebrows pinch together before he answers it. "Hello?" He listens for a second and then holds one finger up to me.

I point to the check out and motion that I'll meet him out front. A quick line, sweet checkout lady, and a few new unisex baby outfits in a bag, I find Brae outside leaning against the wall.

"You ready?" His expression is serious, totally void of his earlier levity. Something about that phone call ripped away his teasing demeanor.

We walk to the Rubicon in silence. I don't want to pry, but I'm worried about Blake. "Was that your brother on the phone?"

He opens the passenger side door and takes my bag to toss it into the backseat. "No."

"Oh." I grab hold of his arm, and he helps to hoist me into the seat. "Have you heard from him?"

His green eyes set on mine and he shakes his head. "No."

Okaaay. Maybe we can try for a two-syllabled answer?

"I'm just worried." I strap on my seatbelt, and before I get out another word, he closes the door and moves around the hood to climb in the driver's seat.

He fires up the engine, but rather than backing out of the spot, he grips the steering wheel then drops his hands and turns to me. "There's something you should know."

Nervous butterflies explode in my stomach.

"The reason Blake went home…what my mom wants to talk to him about is"—he exhales, long and hard—"The General's sick." His shoulders relax a smidge, as if he's been carrying around that secret for a few days too long.

"Sick as in—"

"Cancer, Layla." Pain washes his expression. "He's dying."

My hand flies to my mouth to muffle my cry. I can't speak, but shake my head back and forth slowly as if the movement will toss the truth from my memory.

"The doctors gave him six months tops. He's, uh...even these last few months he's going downhill fast." He rubs his eyes as if he's forcing back tears.

"I'm so sorry." I grip his shoulder and squeeze, hoping to convey comfort. "I...I don't know what to say."

Poor Blake. He thought this trip to see his parents would be their extension of an olive branch, a chance to come back into his life and be grandparents.

He was wrong.

On one hand, I think he'd take that news in stride. He hates his father, and I can see how his death would be upsetting, but I think it would be worse if he had a good relationship with him. On the other hand, the great thing about life is that it gives us plenty of time to make amends for the ways we screwed up. Time allows opportunity for healing. When someone dies suddenly, they no longer have the chance to make things right.

Oh God...Blake.

I sniff back the wave of sadness that overcomes me. I know deep down he wants his father's approval.

"Blake, he's...not okay, is he?" My fingers twist frantically in my hair, itching to comfort him and regretting letting him go.

Braeden's gaze swings to mine. "Honestly?"

I nod.

"No. My mom said he got pretty pissed and took off."

"He's coming home. We need to call him. I bet he jumped on a flight—"

"He's on foot. Left my car in the driveway."

I pat myself down. "Shit. I don't have my phone. Call him, call him right now."

"I tried, Layla. He's not answering."

I breathe deeply, trying to soothe my nerves, regulate my heartbeat, and remind myself that my body isn't my own right now and I owe it to this baby to chill the fuck out.

A dull pain tightens on my left side. I gasp and my hand flies there to push back what's sure to be a baby part pressing against my rib.

"You okay?" His voice is laced with worry.

"Fine, just a big kick." I breathe deeply through the cramp until it subsides. "We need to get back to the condo, just in case Blake shows up."

He nods and points the Rubicon toward home.

"Drive fast."

———

It's almost three p.m. and my phone has rung on the hour every hour since we arrived, but none of the calls were from Blake.

Between pacing and staring blankly at the wall, I've had time to review every possible scenario, and lucky for me I have a vivid imagination. I've closed my eyes and prayed, even willed him to get in touch with me through ESP, but the only person who's been consistently ringing my phone has been Trip.

"Here." Braeden hands me a glass of OJ.

"No thanks, I'm okay—"

"You haven't eaten." His expression is stern, replacing his prettiness with the focus of a hardened soldier. "You need something besides water."

My appetite dissolved. It's as if my stomach is too full of worry to fit anything else in there. But he has a point.

I nod, take the offered juice, and drink as much of it as I can while he's watching. "Thanks."

He takes the glass and brings it to the kitchen. Come on, Blake. He hasn't answered my calls or texts, and somewhere along the way my worry for him has morphed into anger.

"Why won't you pick up your phone and—"

My phone vibrates in my hand. I check the caller ID and hit Accept.

"Blake! Oh my God, are you okay?" A shallow sob bursts from my throat.

"Shhh, Mouse, I'm okay. Are you?" There's a tired panic to his voice that pinches my heart. "I just charged my phone and saw all the missed calls. Is it the baby?"

"I'm fine. I'm fine... I just want to hold you." Another sob.

"Fuck, I want that too. I'm so sorry I didn't get in touch sooner. Brae taking care of you?"

"Yeah, he is, but, Blake, he told me about your dad."

Silence is followed by him clearing his throat. "You're lucky you got the stay-at-home version. The in-your-face version is... *unpleasant.*"

"Are you okay?"

"I am. There's so much I want to tell you, but I want to do it when you're in my arms."

"I'd love that." I check the digital clock on the cable box. "What time does your flight leave?"

"That's, uh...what I wanted to run by you. I'm going to stay the night and come back in the morning."

Disappointment settles in my gut, and the baby must feel it because another tightening kick throttles my side. "Oh, really?"

"If that's okay with you." His words rush out, letting me know he'd put his own needs aside in favor of mine. "If you want me home, I'll jump on the next flight."

"No, that's fine. Just promise me you're okay. The hardest part is knowing you're hurting and that I can't be there for you."

"I'll be okay. I didn't handle the news well, took off for most of the day, and now I have so many fucking questions that I don't think I can move past all the shit I'm feeling without getting some answers."

I have so many fucking questions that I don't think I can move past all the shit I'm feeling without getting some answers.

The single line of truth works like a dagger to the chest. Is that what I need too? Answers that will propel me through the confusion? Help me to put the past behind me for good?

"I think that's smart." *For both of us.*

"Good, thank you, baby. I'll be home around noon tomorrow."

"Okay, Blake. I love you."

"I love you too. Put Brae on the phone for me, yeah?"

I hand the phone to Braeden, who sometime during the conversation had moved to sit next to me on the couch. "He wants to talk to you."

"Bro, what's up?" He drops his head to the back of the couch. "I know, but it's not my news to tell." He regards me for a second. "That's different. She was worried about—" He checks the display screen. "Hold on, dude, Layla's got another call coming in. I'll call you back from my phone."

He hands me the phone and pulls out his own before stepping out to the patio to call Blake back, I assume.

As if on autopilot, I look down.

Unavailable.

I don't think I can move past all the shit I'm feeling without getting some answers.

I hit Accept.

"Trip. How soon can you get to Vegas?"

He stutters. "I can be there tonight."

"I'll see you tomorrow. Eight a.m. Give me your number, and I'll text you the place."

"Sure, yeah…" He gives me the number and I program it into my phone.

"Got it."

"Thank you, thank you, Layla. I just want a chance to explain—"

I hit End before he's finished and mentally prepare for the answers I so desperately need.

And hope that the truth doesn't send my world crashing down around me.

FIFTEEN

BLAKE

I haven't been able to even look at The General since I got back from my anger-induced walkabout and opted for sitting outside rather than risking another confrontation. Although my dad seems to take the hint that I'm avoiding him and leaves me alone, my mom is oblivious.

"Are you sure you don't want to go out to eat?" My mom is sitting with me on the back patio.

"No, Mom, I'm not that hungry."

"You need to eat." Her voice is so timid, just as I remember.

Before I was dragged off in the night to military school, I thought my mom and I had a special bond. I thought she was like me, hiding some secret on the inside to keep it safe while pretending to play the role of perfect wife on the outside. Boy was I wrong.

She didn't keep my secrets out of some bond or loyalty to me. She did it out of fear. Being with Layla has made me see what real strength looks like, and it has zero to do with muscle mass. True strength comes from resilience, an inner force that refuses to give up a fight. It comes in packages of all different sizes, five-foot-three inches of blond and gorgeous with a tongue that can slice through the biggest men with words or bring one to his knees with want.

Funny how weakness can be disguised by strength. On the outside, most would consider my father a strong man, but his unwillingness to fight for his life proves he and my mother are the perfect pair.

"How long has he been sick?" I don't look over at her but keep my focus on the small garden across the yard.

"My guess is it's been awhile. He was having problems but refused to see a doctor."

"Hardheaded son of a bitch." I push two hands through my hair and lock my fingers behind my head.

"Then when all that happened with you in Las Vegas, he changed. He made an appointment, and a few test results later…well, here we are."

I tilt my head to meet her eyes. "Changed after Vegas?"

"Mm. He felt bad, I think, for not believing in you." Her eyes narrow. "He lives with a lot of regret, Blake."

"I highly doubt that. He's hated me from the beginning."

"No, he hasn't. He…" She turns to the back door, probably making sure we're not being overheard, then scoots closer to me. "He sees himself in you."

"God, Mom"—I rub my eyes, pressing in on them until I feel the dull ache in my brain—"don't say that. You're confirming my worst fear by saying that. I'm about to have a baby and make Layla my wife. The last thing I want hanging over my head is the possibility that I'll end up like him."

"I know nothing I say will convince you, but at least give him a chance to explain."

I shake my head, and she leans in closer to catch my eyes. "Please, just talk to him. If you don't like what he has to say, you leave tomorrow and everything goes back to the way it was."

"Until he dies." My stomach pinches painfully.

She clears her throat. "Yes, Blake. Until he dies."

"Fine." I push up from my chair. "Where's he at?"

She blinks up at me a few times. "Bedroom."

I nod and pass by her into the house, heading for my parents' room. Unease pricks at my nerves as I pass by my old bedroom. Everything looks almost exactly the same as it did the night I left. The metal band posters are gone, but the twin bed and dresser are the same.

Reaching my parents' door, I knock softly even though it's cracked. The sound of the local news and the blue light from the television filter through the gap.

"Come in, Son." His voice sounds weak, as if maybe I woke him up.

I push inside to find him on his bed, his back propped up with pillows and a blue blanket over his legs.

"Do you have a second, sir?"

He nods and motions to a chair near his side of the bed before hitting Mute on the TV. "Feel better after getting some air?"

A slight heat warms my cheeks at his witness to my weakness. "Sorry I took off." I tuck my chin and take the offered seat. "I know Mom worries. I just needed to—"

"Process." He regards me with an understanding I've never seen from him before. "I get it. Took *me* three months, so… yeah, I get it."

"And now you've processed?" My fists clench at my thighs. "Come to terms with the fact that you're giving up?" I can't help the anger that floods my veins.

He chuckles softly. "Never really thought about it as giving up. I figured I'd lived a long life. I have no desire to prolong the inevitable if it means my last few months on this earth are spent bedridden. I want to spend my time with your mom, with your brother and you, and I'd like to hold my grandbaby before my time comes"—he drops his chin and smooths his blanket—"if that's okay with you."

Tears sting my eyes, but I force back the emotion and remind myself that this is not the weakened man who sits before me. This is the man who smothered me until I couldn't fight hard enough. This is the man who gave me something to fight for when I should've lived free and easy to do whatever the fuck I wanted.

"Dad, I don't know what to say."

"I'm sorry, Blake. All I ever wanted to do was protect you, and because of that I lost you."

"Protect me from what?" I lean in closer, fixing my glare on his foggy green eyes. "You took everything I loved away from me."

"I know, but that's not how I saw it back then."

"Not how you saw it?" My jaw tenses and I'm spitting words through clenched teeth. "There's no other way to see it."

"What you see, the man I was when you were a growing up…" He sighs heavily and allows a few quiet seconds to tick by. "I wasn't tough when I was a kid. When all the other kids were outside playing, I had my nose shoved in a book. I got teased, beaten up, bullied."

"You never told me that before."

"It was a long time ago." His eyes lose focus and wander away from mine. "It's not something I'm proud of."

"You're not proud of being smart?"

"No, I'm not proud of hating who I was, trying to be like everyone else. I gave up on the books and forced myself into the war games that the other kids were playing. It was hard, but in the end it made life easier." He turns his focused eyes to mine. "I thought I was doing the same for you."

"You could've just sat me down, had a man-to-man."

He drops his salt-n-pepper eyebrows over a steely glare. "Would you have listened to me?"

Fuck, probably not. I hated being told what to do, hated who my dad had become, hid my secret for so long it shoved a wedge between us in a major way.

My non-answer is my answer.

"By that time I was moving up in the ranks, I was powerful, and"—he chuckles—"well, none of that matters. Look at me now." He waves a hand down his once powerful body, which is now still and exhausted. "Dying gives a man a lot of time to think on his mistakes. I don't have a lot of time, but what time I have I want to spend making this up to you."

One wet drop escapes my eye, but I swipe at it before it moves down my cheek. "Make it up to me by fighting. Do whatever it takes to earn us more time. I can't put all these years behind us with only a few months."

"All the treatments take energy, and I'm..." A long breath falls from his lips, and he almost seems to shrink in size. "I'm tired, Blake."

How do I argue that? I've heard cancer treatment is horrific and without hope of survival it would be a daunting prospect. "Will you at least consider it?"

He places his hand on the bed closer to me. It's the nearest he's gotten to physically comforting me, and although he's not even touching me, I feel it. "If anything has ever made me want to fight, it's this moment, the chance to earn your forgiveness. *That's* worth fighting for."

"Fuckin' A, Dad..." I rub my eyes and marvel at the change of events.

So this whole time I've been pissed at The General for fucking up my life, but if he hadn't done what he did, where would I be today?

My stomach hollows out with the realization. He gave me my fight, lit a fire so deep in my gut that I'd crawl through hell if it meant holding on to something I love. My career, Layla,

Axelle, everything I have I had to fight to keep. Holy shit! A wave of gratefulness surges in my chest.

"So." He clears his throat. "Tell me all about Layla, Axelle, and my grandbaby."

Right then it all makes sense.

Everything life throws affects who we become. Different experiences wouldn't have brought me to where I am today. I owe everything I have to the fact that my dad didn't make things easy on me.

Rather than give him my forgiveness, he deserves my gratitude.

SIXTEEN

LAYLA

It's D-Day. Time to hear Trip's side of the story so that I can put my curiosity to rest and end all this before Blake gets back. The phone calls, probing into Axelle's birth records, all of it needs to stop.

I scan my surroundings and try to act casually as I people watch from the small Italian café at The Venetian Hotel. Few Vegas locals hang out at the casinos, which makes this the perfect place to meet without getting caught. The coffee shop is public enough for safety, but I chose a table off in the corner to allow us some privacy.

A warm cup of herbal tea between my hands fights off the chill that I can't seem to shake. It's not lost on me that my hands were cold the last time I saw Trip. I'd be lying if I said I wasn't just as nervous to see Trip today as I was back then, although this time for totally different reasons.

As I wait for the blast from my past to show his face, my thoughts return to Blake. I can't imagine how he must be feeling, and the sooner I get this over with, the sooner I can get to my man and get on with my life. I have every intention of telling Blake about my meeting with Trip, but he's dealing with enough now, and the more I can handle behind his back the better.

He'll be upset, possibly even furious, and insist that these things are his job to handle for me, but he wasn't around the night Axelle was conceived or the nine months afterward when I was treated like a high-school leper. He didn't live with me through sixteen years of abuse and the constant fear that my choices were going to end up destroying my daughter. Nope, that was all me.

Blake was dragged neck deep into my past when Stew showed up at my door. I watched helplessly as he was drugged and jailed all for the sake of loving me. No way I'll risk bringing him down with this shit again.

This has to be the end now, and I won't walk away until I'm convinced it's finally over.

Sitting up straight, unable to relax, I rub a small circle to try to relieve the tightening cramp in my side. My lower back seemed to spasm all night, or maybe it was junior working out some kickboxing moves. Either way I can't seem to shake the feeling that this baby is getting way too big for my body.

I take another gander through the small coffee shop, swiveling on my stool. A couple, some people in business suits, and a small group of girls, but still no Trip.

My eyes scan the area back and forth, unable to shake the feeling that somehow Braeden knows I'm up to no good. I told him this morning I was meeting up with some girls to walk for exercise and that he wouldn't want to come and listen to them talk about menstrual cycles and yeast infections. After he recovered from gagging, he let me go, as long as I promised to text him when I got here, which I did, and before I leave, which I will.

A tall man with short brown hair, the color of milk chocolate, enters the café, stops, and immediately locks eyes with me.

Trip Miller.

His sky-blue eyes widen for a second before he continues toward me. I study him as he approaches. His worn jeans fit nicely on his long legs, a black long-sleeved collared shirt is left untucked and rolled up to his elbows, and as he gets closer, I can see part of a tattoo that curls up the left side of his neck. Although his hair isn't as shaggy as it was in high school, it's spiky in a way that still gives him an edge, and his face is still as handsome, but now more rugged and grown up.

The sight of him used to send my stomach tumbling in a flurry of butterflies, but now there's nothing but simple appreciation and anxiety.

He stands at the edge of the table and blows out a deep breath with his hand on his chest. "Layla, wow…you look great."

"Thanks, um…" I motion to the seat across from me. "Have a seat."

He pulls out the stool and sits, the waitress on his heels to take his order. "Coffee, black."

After she disappears to grab his drink, he turns to me. "Thank you for meeting with me."

"You didn't really give me much choice." I thumb the ceramic handle of my mug. "How did you get my number?"

"The receptionist at the UFL Training Center." His cheeks take on color and he ducks his chin, clearly embarrassed over his stalking behavior.

"Vanessa." That bitch.

"Um, yeah, sorry about that." He peeks up. "You're pregnant." His eyes dart to my ring finger, and I'm grateful to have Blake's engagement ring on so he doesn't get the impression that I make a habit out of getting knocked up out of wedlock, which I do. "How many kids do you have?"

"This'll be my second."

The waitress delivers his coffee, but Trip doesn't take a sip, only cups it in his hands as I'm doing with my tea. Silence stretches between us, and a sense of urgency to get what I need, call Trip off his interest in me and Axelle, and get home to welcome Blake back rides me hard.

"Listen, Trip, I don't mean to rush this, but—"

"Cut to the chase." His lips form a tight line, as if he's disappointed that we won't be skipping down memory lane holding hands for a while longer.

"Please."

His knuckles go white around his coffee, and he fixes his eyes on mine, but doesn't offer a word.

Great. I guess I'll lead. "About the night at the party, you have to understand I remember very little. After hearing from Stewart that…I was raped…"

He cringes and rubs the back of his neck, but doesn't confirm or deny it.

"I thought not remembering was a blessing, but after talking to you, there are missing pieces, and I have to know if anything Stew told me was even true."

His expression hardens. "Fuckin' hate that guy."

I flash him what's sure to be a weak smile. "You're not alone in that, I assure you."

He finally sips his coffee then sets it down, staring into it. "I had my speech planned out, thought through everything I was going to say, and now that I'm here, I don't know where to start."

I lean forward, my forearms braced on the table. "How 'bout the beginning?"

He nods, takes another sip of his coffee, and then leans back in his chair. "I had a shitty upbringing. My stepdad was a prick. He'd slap me around, get drunk, and make my mom cry. I was kind of rebellious. I'm sure you noticed."

"Yeah, I did." It's one of the things I adored about him.

"I liked you freshman year, but always thought you were too good, too, uh…sweet for a guy like me. Sophomore year came then junior, and as every year passed, I became more obsessed." He shrugs. "You really stood out."

He was obsessed? *I* was the one who was obsessed. "You never even spoke to me."

"I know. You scared me. There was something about you, even just the way you looked, that intimidated the hell out of me. You were so confident."

Huh…I guess I was, back then, before Stew.

"Anyway, when you showed up at that party, dressed like a rock-n-roll princess, I knew I was done for. I couldn't resist you any longer. I drank, trying to build up the courage to talk to you. Seeing you hanging out with Stew and all his fucking losers just drove me to drink more. I hated seeing his arm on your shoulder, his eyes eating you up when you weren't looking." He looks down and I follow his gaze to see his knuckles go white gripping his mug. "I wanted to pull you away from him."

A shiver runs up my spine at the menace in his voice. "Did you?"

His cobalt eyes find mine. "I didn't have to. You came to me."

I blink, trying to crank back in my memory and remember. I wanted to talk to him that night, told myself I wasn't going to leave until I did, but don't recall actually doing it.

"I knew you were pretty wasted, but I had no clue just how wasted you were until…" He turns away, his face flushed. "Until later."

I sift my hand into my hair at my nape and massage the back of my neck, trying to recall that night. "I don't remember any of that. I must've made a total fool of myself."

"Not at all." He wipes something invisible off the tabletop. "You were sweet. We talked about music and cars, Mrs. Caffrey's wig."

A tiny grin ticks my lips. "Her wig was hideous."

"It really was." He chuckles, but his laughter dies when his eyes meet mine. "We were talking and laughing. Then out of nowhere you just leaned in, wrapped your arms around my neck, pushed up on your tiptoes, and kissed me."

My cheeks flame and I duck my chin. "Oh wow, I'm, uh... I'm sorry."

"Don't be." He tilts his head, his eyes on my lips. "I loved it."

Why does reliving this now feel like cheating? He couldn't possibly have feelings for me now, nine months pregnant with another man's baby and his ring on my finger.

I bury my face in my tea and take a long sip.

He shakes his head and blinks. "Anyway, one thing led to another, and it was like the more we kissed the more we needed. Two years of pent-up feelings mixed with liquor, and I was helpless to stop it."

The baby does what feels like a backbend, and I try to rub away a low cramp. "And by 'it' you mean...?"

"We found an empty room in the house. I swear I didn't plan to let things get as far as they did. I just wanted to get you alone for a little while, kiss you without an audience, but when I tried to slow down"—he shakes his head, a tiny smile curling his lips—"you told me you loved me."

I groan and drop my head into my hands. God, that's totally something I'd do. I was so infatuated with him I'm sure I did that.

A soft chuckle calls my eyes to his. "Hey, don't be embarrassed. It was amazing. I mean..." He shakes his head, his eyebrows dropped low with the seriousness of whatever he's about to say. "No one in my life had ever loved me, and there I was locked in a dark room with this gorgeous girl who has awesome taste in music, and she *loved* me. I can't tell you how long I held on to that."

That's sweet in a sad way. "I don't understand. How could I have been aware enough to do all this, but not remember?"

"I didn't say you didn't slur it." He shrugs one shoulder. "You were stumbling and giggling. It wasn't until about halfway through that I realized you were—God, this is so humiliating." He runs one big hand over his face.

"We've come this far, Trip." As much as I don't want to be witness to my teenage self's embarrassment, I have to know. "Might as well put it all out there."

"I didn't have a lot of experience back then. I was pretty fucked up myself, but looking back on it, I'm pretty sure you were slipping in and out of consciousness."

I cringe. "That's awful."

"By the time it was over, you were out. I didn't know what to do. I tried to wake you up, but you were totally gone. I checked to make sure you were breathing, heart was still beating, but I panicked. I dressed you as best I could, pulled the covers up over you, and tried to figure out what the fuck to do." His hand fists into his hair as if he's reliving that night eighteen years ago. "I sat there for what felt like hours when someone knocked on the door. It was that girl, the one I'd seen you talking to earlier."

Oh shit, what was her name? "Daphne…"

"Yeah." He nods. "I think she figured out pretty quickly what had gone on. She seemed…I don't know…worried about you? Or concerned? I wanted to get you out of there, get you home, but I couldn't exactly carry you out of there unconscious and thrown over my shoulder."

Dread drops like a rock in the pit of my stomach. "What did you do, Trip?" The words drift from my lips on a whisper, something inside already well aware of what he did.

Pain slices through his expression. "She said she'd take care of you." He swallows hard. "Told me she'd stay with you until you woke up, make sure you got home okay."

"Oh my God." I drop my forehead into my hand and groan.

Daphne hated me. Even after that night, she had nothing but contempt for me as if my being with Stewart robbed her of her plan to seduce and marry the asshole.

"I'm so sorry." His voice shakes with emotion, but I feel nothing for his pain. "I really thought she'd take care of you."

I rub my temples and search for a feeling, a memory, something that validates his story. "She didn't."

"Fuck, Layla." His eyes darken in a scary way. "I never should've left you."

"I can't believe this shit. She was in on it." Fuck! "Why you didn't tell me this sooner? We had an entire year together, and you wouldn't even look at me."

"At first, I tried. When I'd pass by you in the hallway, you'd always have your eyes to the floor. After that night, you weren't the same girl."

"You took my virginity, Trip." My whispered shriek sends him back in his chair as if it delivered a physical blow. "I wasn't the same girl."

"I'm so sorry, I know, and I deserve your anger." His pleading gaze fixes on mine. "I broke you. I could see it. I assumed that you'd woken the next day hating me for leaving you after having unprotected sex with you. You'd have every right to. And then you were hanging out with Stewart every day. I never saw you again by yourself. You were always with him."

I dig the heels of my palms into my forehead, pushing back the headache that's starting to form behind my eyes. "Still, when you realized I was pregnant, you had to have wondered."

"I didn't wonder." His jaw is hard. "I knew."

He knew? My jaw falls loose on its hinges. He fucking knew!

My blood ignites with the heat of my anger. "Why didn't you say anything? Do you have any idea what he put me through? What he put Axelle through? You had the power to save us!"

He leans in, eyebrows low. "I had nothing to offer you. Stew had his father's fucking legacy. I had a drug-addict mom and a stepdad who knocked me around. I thought by letting you go I was doing what was best for you and our baby."

I lean in, pinning him with a glare. "You were wrong."

"Why the fuck do you think I'm here?"

"Now? You show up now, eighteen years later? It was you who checked Axelle's birth records and my divorce records, wasn't it?"

His chest puffs out. "Yes."

"Why?" I take a deep breath through another slight cramp. Blake would kill me for allowing myself to endure this kind of stress. I need to relax, if not for me, for the baby. For Blake.

"After the news broke about what Stewart did to that fighter and the gossip back home carried its way to me, I'd realized that I fucked up. But Layla, you don't know the life I've had. I wasn't fit to be a father, a husband, or even a friend. After my mom moved me to Oregon, I lost it. I hated knowing that you were out there raising my baby and I was so far away."

"Didn't hate it enough to come searching for us," I say through gritted teeth.

"I was in prison for ten years for armed robbery." He recoils at his own words, as if they came out without his permission.

I gasp and try to slam my lips closed, but I'm too late to stop it.

"Look, I don't know what happened with Stew and his crew of fuckheads after I left, but I do know that what happened between us meant something. Axelle was created by two people in love. Maybe not a conventional love, but Layla, I haven't stopped thinking about you once since then."

The power of his words, the sincerity in his eyes, all of it is sweet, but I don't know if I felt the same even back then. I had a crush, a really intense crush, but as soon as I found out I was pregnant, I didn't think much about Trip Miller. My baby was all I cared about, she became my world, and I relinquished all my own dreams to make sure she was taken care of.

"What are you saying?"

He licks his lips and seems to think carefully about what he's going to say next. "I know I'm too late." He nods to my ring finger and then to my swollen belly. "I'd hoped there could be a future for us—maybe we could get to know each other again and see what happens—but now all I ask is to know my daughter."

"I'm sorry. I can't give you that." I push my tea away, suddenly repulsed by the smell or maybe just sick of all I'm hearing. "She knows everything, Trip. She was there the night Stew confessed."

He recoils. "Fuck…really?"

"She wants nothing to do with her biological father. She thinks he's a rapist."

His mouth twists in disgust. "Do you think you could talk to her for me? Let her know that…tell her our story."

"My fiancé has legally adopted Axelle."

He drops his head into his hands with a mumbled "Shit."

"I'm sorry."

His head still in his hands, face to the table, he nods and sniffs.

My heart breaks a little at seeing him like this, but he should've come forward sooner. Sometimes amends come too late.

"So that's it then?" He rubs his eyes with his thumb and forefinger. "I've lost you both."

"Can't lose what you never had."

He lifts his head, his eyes bloodshot and watery. "Right." I can tell he's pissed, but what was he expecting? To breeze into our lives and have us run into his open arms?

"I appreciate you coming all the way out here to explain, and I'm sorry I don't have better news for you, but I need to get back."

He curls his lips between his teeth, avoids my eyes, and nods.

It takes me a few seconds to hoist myself down from the stool. I grab my bag and study the side of Trip's face. No one in his right mind would need a paternity test to see that he's Axelle's father. His profile is a masculine version of hers, coloring identical. A sharp pain twists in my chest and another in my side.

I breathe a few times until it lets up then rest my hand on his shoulder. "I wish you the best."

He doesn't reply, and I turn my back on Trip, on the past, and refuse to give it another second of my time.

A sense of freedom overwhelms me as I exit the café. I'm grateful I got the story of how Axelle came to be. Chances are the other stuff Stewart spewed happened after Trip left, but at least I know that my daughter was brought into this world under better circumstances. I willingly lost my virginity to Trip Miller and made a baby. I can live with that. And I think Axelle can too.

I move through the hotel, ambling along the man-made river where gondolas filled with tourists glide slowly across the water. Another cramp hits me, this one harder than the last. I grip the railing that runs along the river and breathe in…out… Shit! This one is lasting longer than the others. In…out…in…I blow out a long breath, and a soft breeze of air conditioning against my face brings my hand to my forehead. I'm sweating?

This can't be labor. Can it?

Just breathe, get to the valet, and get home.

I take a deep breath and test my legs to make sure they're steady before I start moving again. Although the cramp is gone, there's an awareness that I haven't felt until now. Maybe I'm overreacting, but I can't help but feel as if another cramp is coming.

"It's okay. My water hasn't broken. Until then, I'm fine." I keep whispering my pep-talk as I follow the river's edge to the casino.

Weaving through the tables and machines, another cramp hits me. "Holy fucking shit!" My jaw locks hard, my entire belly tightening up so much that I can't take a full breath. I brace myself against a stool at a roulette table.

"Ma'am, are you okay?"

I don't know who said it, the dealer or maybe someone at the table. I wave and force a smile. "Fine. I'm fine."

I try to move on, my goal to get somewhere private to grab my phone and call Braeden, but two steps and I'm holding onto another stool.

"Fuck, Layla!" Strong hands grip my shoulders and pull me up. "Shit, you need to go to the hospital."

Trip? I peer up at his face. "Are you following me?" A cramp twists in my gut, and I fall limply to his chest.

"No, I saw you stagger when you left." He hooks his hands under my arms to hold me up. "So I followed—okay, so yeah, I followed you but only because I was worried."

Blake would hate this. I need to get in touch with Brae. I push off of Trip, but it's weak. "I'm okay. I just need to get ho—"

Warm moisture drops from between my legs, slowly bleeding down my inner thighs and soaking my yoga pants.

I tilt my head back and stare into Trip's worried blue eyes. "My water just broke."

SEVENTEEN

BLAKE

"Thank you for choosing FlyWest, and welcome to Las Vegas." The stewardess' announcement couldn't come soon enough. I've been crazed with getting back home to Layla to tell her about the breakthrough I had with my dad over the weekend.

After a long-drawn-out conversation last night, we ordered pizza and sat around while my parents listened to me talk. I told them about my music room and how long I'd had it hidden and explained that Layla was the first person I let in and how we fell in love. I gave them all the details that they didn't know about Stew's arrest and my legally adopting Axelle. It was midnight before I noticed how tired they both looked and insisted we finish in the morning.

And we did over breakfast.

They're planning on coming to town when the baby is born. My dad is still healthy enough to travel, but my guess is if he chooses not to get treatment, this'll be the last time he comes to visit.

The plane taxis to our gate, and my leg is thumping double time with the urge the break out of here. I texted my brother before we took off, telling him that it was on time, and he said he'd be waiting at the curb.

With my woman.

I lick my lips with anticipation, hoping we have the condo to ourselves for a few hours so I can show Layla just how much I missed her. Nothing sounds better than stripping down and holding her to me. There's no better feeling in the world than having a naked Layla in my bed. It's not even about the sex; although, when we get naked, that's pretty much inevitable.

The fasten seatbelt sign is off, and I'm up and hunched over in the tiny aisle as the people filter from the plane. Once in the airport, I power walk past the baggage claim and through the sliding glass doors.

My eyes scan left, right, but I don't see the Rubicon. I check my phone. I'm ten minutes late. Maybe they drove around and are coming back—

"Blake!"

I whirl around toward Axelle's voice.

She's stepping out of an old Jeep Wrangler. That's Killer's car. Why the hell is he picking me up?

"Hey, kiddo!"

She runs up to me, and the closer she gets, the clearer I can see the panic in her eyes. "It's Mom. She's in labor."

My heart drops into my stomach, adrenaline floods my veins, and my hands fist at my sides. "What!"

"Come on. I'll explain in the car."

We jog to Killer's Jeep, and Axelle jumps in the back while I hop in the front. "Talk. Now."

"I was home and Braeden was waiting for mom to get home."

"Home from where? Why wasn't Brae with her?"

"I don't know. But he got a call from some guy who said he was with Mom and she'd gone into labor."

I turn my body around as much as I can and face Axelle. "What the fuck did you just say?"

"Mom went into labor at The Venetian, and some guy she was having coffee with took her to the hospital."

My eyes squint so hard they twitch. Anger settles deep in my gut as I make a mental list of who I'm going kill first: Braeden, then this asshole who has my woman, and then after Layla's finished birthing our baby, she's got some fucking explaining to do. Why the hell didn't she stay with my brother as I fucking asked her to?

"Don't go there, man." Killian's voice calls over to me even though his eyes are on maneuvering us through the Vegas streets. "She's with your brother now. I'm sure she can explain."

He's right, but that doesn't change the fact that I want some fucking answers.

"Oh my God, we're having a baby!" Axelle's high-pitched squeal and her grip on my shoulder ignite my excitement.

Fuckin A. We're having a baby. "Drive faster, Killer."

"Got it." He lays heavy on the gas and soon we pull up to the emergency entrance of the hospital.

My heart pounds in my chest to the point that I'm dizzy. It wasn't long ago I walked through these same doors the day Sadie was born. How Jonah held himself together through that, I'll never know.

We all jump from the Jeep and jog to the front desk.

"Layla Moorehead. She's in labor. We're her family." Axelle's practically jumping.

"Hey, you can't park your car there," a security guard says and moves toward us.

The front desk nurse glances up at us. "Room 323, Labor and Delivery." She stands and leans over the desk. "It's right down—"

"Thank you!" Axelle calls out her gratitude from behind me as I'm halfway down the hallway.

"Hey, the car!" The security guy must be talking to Killer.

I hear him toss the keys and the sound of them hitting the tile floor. "Here, keep 'em!"

Axelle and Killer catch up to me as we zigzag our way through the hospital, following the signs and arrows that lead us to Labor and Delivery.

We rush up to another desk with a young nurse sitting behind it. "Hi, I'm Blake Daniels, here for Layla. I'm the father."

Her eyes brighten. "Oh, yeah. They're expecting you." She hits a few keys on her computer. "You can go on back."

"Thanks." I turn to Axelle, who nods, a huge grin on her face. "This is it, kiddo. We're having a baby."

She nods again and claps her hands. "Okay."

I kiss the top of her head.

"A-Axelle?" A man's voice calls from a small couch in the waiting room.

We swivel our heads in unison toward the voice.

Older guy, dark hair, decent size. He takes a tentative step toward her, his eyes wide in shock. I can't explain why, whether it's the eerie way he's staring at my girl, or the strange familiarity of his face, but tension scents the air.

She leans into me ever so slightly. "Do I know you?"

The man blinks a few times and moves closer.

"Stop right there." The low growling command comes from Killer, who's now flanking Axelle on her other side.

The guy stops, his gaze bouncing between the three of us as if he can't figure out what to make of us.

"Who the fuck are you?" If he knows Axelle, I have to assume that this douchebag knows Layla.

"You must be Blake." He tilts his head, studying me.

He's not in bad shape, about my height, maybe a few inches shorter. He looks as if he's probably one of those outdoorsy guys who hike and swim laps. If push came to shove, I'd destroy the pansy.

I take step toward him, and he doesn't back down. Gotta give him credit for that. "You know me. I'll give you one more chance to tell me who the fuck you are and why you're addressing my daughter like you know her."

"Your daughter." He laughs in a way that's less humor more teasing.

I shove him hard, and he rocks back on one foot.

"Blake." Braeden pushes through the double doors, appearing in my peripheral vision. "Stop." He steps between us, his back to me. "Trip, man, back the fuck off my brother. I told you to go home."

Trip? Why does that name sound familiar?

The guy, Trip, motions to Axelle. "I just wanted to meet my daughter."

A gasp flies from Axelle's lips a second before Killer descends. His fist flies, cracking Trip in the jaw and knocking him on his ass.

"Killian!" Axelle rushes up and attempts to grab him from behind.

He holds her back, gently, but firmly. "You fucking dare show your face around here, motherfucker!" Killer charges again, this time caught up by Brae.

"Calm down!" He jerks Killer hard. "You hear me? Stand the fuck down. This is not helping Layla."

My eyes move between a stunned Axelle and a dazed Trip. Holy shit…she looks just like the guy. Prettier, more feminine, but yeah, that's her biological father.

Oh hell no!

A guttural roar rumbles from my chest and I lunge. "You sick son of a bitch!" I slam my fist into his jaw, making contact with a sickening crack. "You've been snooping." Another solid hit to his jaw. "Shoulda' stayed away." I throw another punch, but I'm pulled back by Killer and Brae before I make contact. I thrash, trying to break free, fear and anger swirling in my blood to destroy the man who raped my woman. The man who's been digging around through birth records and now *stalking* my family.

"We got this, bro. We'll take care of him." Brae yells in my ear. "Don't get escorted out of here and miss the birth of your baby, man. Get your shit together and go help your woman!"

"Don't let that motherfucker go," I growl.

"Got it. Now go." Brae shoves me off toward the door.

I glare at the bleeding piece of shit on the floor and point right at him. "I'm not even close to being done with you." I hook an arm around a whimpering Axelle. "Come on, kiddo. The boys'll deal with him. Let's go bring our baby into the world."

EIGHTEEN

LAYLA

"As soon as the doctor gets here, we'll start pushing." Danita, my nurse who's been here with me since I checked in, squeezes my hand and gives me a kind smile.

I nod, exhausted, in pain, and incapable of speech.

Why in the holy hell did I refuse the drugs? I wanted to experience labor since I didn't get to when I had Axelle. I'd read so many birthing books that didn't make it sound this hard. Fucking liars! My lower back muscles have been in a constant state of contraction, and my womb is not far behind.

Danita holds my hand between hers, her head turned to the monitor. "Here comes another one, Layla."

I want to roar, "No shit, I can feel it!" but instead roll my lips between my teeth and prepare.

She leans down and fixes her eyes with mine. "Relax. Focus. Now breathe."

My fingers grip the edge of the bed as another wave of contractions hits me hard. Every muscle in my abdomen pulls tight, tighter, so tight they feel twisted, as if they're about to break or rip right through my skin. I bite down, holding back the moan of agony that pushes at my throat.

"Almost done. Keep breathing. You're doing great."

I gasp for air. Having forgotten to breathe, my head feels light. Sweat breaks out over my skin. My eyes pinch closed. God, make it stop.

"Layla, shit…"

I open my eyes to Blake, who's standing on the other side of the bed, Axelle at his side.

Just seeing them here causes tears to spring free from my eyes, and a guttural sob rips from my chest.

Blake moves in, grabbing my other hand and pulls it to his chest before burying his face in my neck. "Sh, sh…" His lips move against my skin, small kisses between his talking. "I'm here, baby. I've got you. Sh…"

Slowly the contraction fades, and I take a long deep breath of relief and try to sink back onto the bed.

"Blake, right?" Danita smiles warmly at him.

He straightens but doesn't release my hand while he rubs circles against my skin nervously. "Yeah, yes. Blake."

If I weren't so tired, I'd smile.

"Nice to meet you." Her gaze swings to Axelle. "And you must be the big sister."

"Yes, Axelle." She throws up a tiny finger wave.

"Axelle, why don't you come take my spot. You guys got here just in time for her to push." Danita places my sweaty hand into Axelle's, and I grin up at my daughter as she peers down at me.

Her eyes sparkle with tears, but they're red, as if she's been crying.

I pull her hand up and kiss it. "Honey? I'm okay." I regard Blake, who's staring intently at Axelle. Something passes between them. "Guys, I'm fine." My eyes narrow on Blake. "What's going on?"

He seems to shake off whatever it was he was thinking, and his soft stare bores into mine. "Besides the fact that we're having a baby?" A tiny smile curls his lips.

Did Braeden tell Blake about Trip? I made him promise he wouldn't until after the baby is born so I could tell him myself. No, surely Brae wouldn't do that to his own brother.

The sound of voices at the door makes me glimpse over to see Danita putting on a long gown, rubber gloves, and a mask. "Doctor's here." I can't see her mouth, but the smile in her eyes says it all.

It's time to have the baby.

I grip Blake's and Axelle's hands tighter, excitement and absolute terror warring behind my ribs.

"Aw shit," Blake growls. "You've gotta be kidding me." His hand gets tight.

I look up and follow his gaze to the entrance of my room where Dr. Cole is standing, shaking his head.

"…another contraction…" A random nurse mumbles.

"Mr. Daniels, it seems the fates are against you." Dr. Cole moves into the room, already dressed in scrubs, and a few nurses busy to get him in a gown while he pulls on gloves.

A low groan vibrates from Blake's chest, and I yank on his arm. It's weak, but it's enough to get his attention. "Blake, it's okay. Let's just—*Argh!*"

The contraction grips me from what seems like out of nowhere. "Holy shit…" I squeeze their hands, and the doctor takes his place along with the nurses. I'm lost in the pain of my contraction but feel my legs being placed into stirrups and the heat of a warm light between my legs.

I don't need to look at Blake to know he's probably shooting daggers at the doctor who has a front row seat to every damn thing between my legs. Oh well, he can get the fuck over it, or *he* can push a human out of *his* body if he wants a say.

A low groan rolls from my chest out my mouth, and Blake jerks then swings his eyes to mine.

"Breathe, baby…" His tender voice combined with the feel of his hot breath against my neck calms me a little, even though my womb is still intent on squeezing this baby out.

"Alright, guys," Dr. Cole addresses Axelle and Blake. "When it's time to push, I want you to hook your elbow beneath the leg you're standing closest to. Pull it back and count with us."

Axelle nods. "Okay."

Blake tightens his glare aimed back at the doctor.

The doc rolls his eyes and focuses his attention down low. "Alright, Layla, I can feel the baby's head. When this next contraction hits, I want you to push, okay? Don't push with your face. Push with your abdomen, got it?"

I nod and try to relax during my brief reprieve.

"Blake, are you good?" I can't put my finger on it, but something seems off about him. It's not the interaction with the doctor; it's something else. He looks…sick.

He turns his pale face to me, licks his lips, and nods.

"I can't believe this!" Axelle's voice is laced with pure joy and excitement. "I'm getting a brother or sister today!"

I squeeze her hand, but as the tightening creeps up, I can already tell this one is going to be huge. My eyes find Dr. Cole's, and he checks the monitor and then nods. "Here it comes, Layla. You ready?"

Blake and Axelle hook an arm under each of my knees, and at the doc's okay, they both pull back as the contraction shreds through me. I push, hard, as I've never pushed before because I know the second I get this baby out the sooner I can be done.

"Good, push…three…four…five…six…seven…" Everyone in the room counts in unison.

There's a fullness between my legs, a burning, stretching sensation. Every muscle, even my neck and fingers, get wobbly with the force of my strain.

"Good, Layla, keep pushing." The doctor busies his hands between my legs, but I can't see what he's doing beyond my belly.

The contraction fades, and I crash back into the bed.

"Looks like you've got a tow head." Danita rubs my foot soothingly.

"That's some pretty blond baby hair." Dr. Cole says and then glances up at the monitor.

"Wait, what?" Blake's eyes pass among everyone who is getting the VIP show to my vagina, looking for clarification. "Hair?"

They nod, and Dr. Cole, after a few beats of silence, motions for Blake to go see. "Yeah, come take a look."

Blake kisses my hand and then my forehead, silently asking permission for him to leave me.

"Yes, go see our baby."

BLAKE

I move around Layla, stunned, wobbly, and—fuck, I'm dizzy. I blink and stand over the doctor's shoulder while a masked nurse takes my old spot at Layla's knee.

Blinking, I stare between Layla's legs, and—oh wow—I suck in air through my mouth and lock my knees to keep them from shaking.

They weren't kidding. Coming out of my woman's body, which now looks very little like what I'm used to seeing, is the top of a head, blood-smeared and covered in some kind of guck with a mess of golden hair. Even though it looks like something out of a horror flick, warmth swells behind my ribs.

"Here comes another one, Layla." Dr. Cole, who under the circumstances is as cool as a fucking cucumber, gently pulls at the skin around the baby's head. "Get ready to push. Give me all you can, okay? We're almost there."

"Oh, God…" Layla's whimpered words dissolve on a growl as she bears down. Axelle and the nurse bring her knees to her armpits.

My stomach tumbles, and I'm locked on the tiny head that slowly emerges from her body, inch by inch, until—my leg gives, but I lock it out and avoid bracing myself against the doc's back.

Lord knows he's got enough to deal with.

"Mom, breathe." Axelle coaches her mom, who listens by blowing out a long breath before sucking it back in and grunting through a push.

The room fills with voices, but they all blend together in a symphony of chaos, encouraging and counting. And then the head is out. Oh my God!

Dr. Cole turns my baby's head, and a fierce growl tries to push from my chest, but the noise never makes it to the surface. I'm stuck, locked on the first glimpse of that tiny face.

My breath catches in my throat. Beautiful…the most beautiful thing I've ever seen. A nurse hands the doc what looks like a tiny turkey baster, and I blink hard, trying to focus.

Blood, suction, and then the sound: a tiny whisper of a baby noise.

The room spins. Black darkens the edge of my vision. My head goes light and I lose my legs.

"Man down!" The voice sounds so far away. "We've got a fainter…"

NINETEEN

LAYLA

A huge thud reverberates through the room.

"Man down!" A nurse rushes to where Blake used to be. "We've got a fainter."

"Blake?" It's all I get out before the contraction tightens again. I cry out, digging my nails into the bed.

"Here's the big push, Layla!" The doctor's busy; his shoulders move as he assists in getting the baby out of my body. Danita stands beside him with an open blanket.

Oh my God, this is it!

"Blake!" I call for him through a throaty snarl and try to push up to see him.

"He's fine, Layla." The doctor's urgent voice calls me back. "You need to concentrate."

I channel all my worry for Blake into my gut and give one final push—one final burn so deep and intense I cry out—and then the pressure is gone. I fall back onto the bed, panting, trying to keep my eyes open. The sweet sound of my baby's cry fills the room and tears leak out to stream down my face.

Blake's up, wobbling and holding back nurses. "I'm okay, dammit!" He sounds almost drunk as he staggers to occupy his spot behind the doctor.

Axelle rushes over to him, dipping under his armpit to hold him up. He takes her support, even though, because of his size, she couldn't keep him standing if she had to.

Her eyes are red and tearing as she stares in wide-eyed wonder. "Mom…" Her hands cover her mouth and her shoulders shake in silent sobs.

"Congratulations." Danita places the naked and goo-covered baby to my chest. "It's a boy."

Blake rushes to my side, Axelle in tow but now no longer holding him up. "A boy." His whisper is reverent and filled with so much emotion that the power of it breaks through the pain and straight to my soul.

My gown hangs loose around my neck, and our newborn son nuzzles against my bare chest and falls asleep. His tiny warm body presses against my skin, and my heart explodes with love: love for my life and all the amazing things I've fought so hard to keep.

"Hey, little man." Blake's big hand covers our son. "God, Mouse…" His voice cracks, and I catch sight of a single tear as it falls down his cheek. He makes no attempt to wipe it away, wearing the love for his son like a badge of honor. "He's perfect." His eyes, so much greener now and filled with love, lock onto mine. He places a tender kiss on my lips, and I taste the saltiness of another tear gliding off his powerful jaw. "Thank you. I'll never be able to thank you enough for this gift."

I sniff back the emotion and place a free hand on his cheek. "I know exactly how you feel."

He closes his eyes for a brief moment before he leans down and covers our son's head, face, and shoulder with kisses, not at all concerned with the gooey film. "I love you. I'll always love you." More kisses. "You're perfect, Son. No matter what you end up being"—he clears his throat—"I'll love you."

Axelle whimpers and he reaches out to her. "Shit, kiddo." He sniffs. "Come here, babe."

She's bawling and tucks under Blake's arm, her hand going to rest on her little brother.

Blake kisses the top of her head. "I love you, Axelle Rose. I love you just as much as I love your brother. Understand?"

A sob rips from her chest, and she turns into his body. "I love you too."

More tears erupt until we're all crying and touching, whispering words of reassurance to each other.

This is what life is all about. It's these moments, these few hours of euphoric joy that make up for years and years of torture.

Love.

Love is what makes the pain of the fight so worth it.

—

BLAKE

Things have mellowed out. We've all cried, and, fuck, I hadn't cried in forever. After we all watched the baby get his first bath and a nurse assured us that Trip had been taken away and hasn't been back, Axelle ran out to get Brae and Killian.

Trip is something we need to talk about, but now isn't the time.

I'm mesmerized as Layla has our son to her breast. My chest feels tight at the beauty of watching the woman I love feed our baby from her body. There's nothing more miraculous in the world. I'm on a high, floating above the world on a rush ten times better than anything life has ever given me. Better than fighting, my music, all of it.

I push a strand of hair from Layla's eyes, and she tilts her head up. "He's so sweet, Blake."

"Yeah…" I run my thumb along her lower lip. "Just like you."

Her cheeks flush and she smiles. "We need to name him."

"I got nothing. I swore he was a girl, so I hadn't even considered boy names." I dip down and press a kiss onto his beanie-covered head, eliciting a tiny baby grunt that sounds a lot like *back off, I'm eating.* "Sorry, bud."

"I was thinking since I got to name Axelle you should name him." Her face scrunches. "But um…I'd avoid naming him after any members of your favorite bands."

"Well crap." I fix my eyes on the ceiling and shake my head. "You're saying I have to abandon the dream of a son named Lars Ulrich Daniels?"

A tiny giggle vibrates her chest. "Yes. That's exactly what I'm saying."

Hmm…I stare at his tiny face poking out of the human blanket burrito he's wrapped up in. He's feisty, strong, destined to be insanely handsome. My lips curl into a grin. Above all that, he's heroic. His life alone is healing Layla's heart and my relationship with my dad. Hell, even Axelle seems soothed in her brother's presence. What name encapsulates all that?

"How about Jackson?"

She lifts an eyebrow, peeking up at me from under her long eyelashes. "As in Michael?"

"No, as in Braeden Jackson Daniels." Yeah, hearing the name from my lips, I know it fits.

Layla studies our now-sleeping son. "Are you a Braeden Jackson?" A warm smile softens her expression even more. "We could call him Jack."

"A fighter named Jack, guitar player named Jack, ballet dancer named Jack, they all work."

She tilts her head back, hitting me with a smile that just about drops me to my knees, all soft and gooey and full of love. "It's perfect."

"You sure you're okay naming him after my brother?"

"Of course. After all, he was here for the better part of my labor and—oh, Blake!" She shakes her head, her hand coming over her mouth. "I have so much to tell you."

"Shh…" I run my hand over her hair, which's a tangled mess. "It's okay. I know about Trip."

Her eyes pop wide. "You do? But ho—"

"You really wanna do this now?" I tuck a strand behind her ear.

The burn that should flare at the mention of Axelle's biological father is absent. Nothing could touch the high I'm on. Maybe now is the best time to talk about it.

"I didn't mean to go behind your back, but you were dealing with all that stuff with your family, and Trip wouldn't let up. I just wanted to put everything behind us so we could move forward, ya know?"

She goes on to explain the Unavailable calls, Eve's picking up the call, and realizing it was Trip. I can understand why his contacting her was intriguing enough to seek more information. Looks like ole Stew wasn't totally forthcoming that day in Layla's apartment when he spewed all that bullshit about how Axelle was conceived. Fucking asshole piece of shit.

"And then I went into labor. He was there, saw me, threw me in a cab, and called Brae." She shrugs, and I can hear the heaviness from fear of what could've happened in her voice.

I'm still not happy about that assface showing up to talk to my woman, but he helped her when she needed it. I cringe inwardly. "Shit." I run my hand over my head. "Guess I owe the guy an apology for the beating, eh?"

"Beating!" Her hand shoots out to grip my forearm. "What did you do?"

I have a hard time meeting her eyes, not wanting to show her my guilt. "I, uh…may've expressed my irritation at him showing up and confronting Axelle with a little fist-to-face therapy."

She's silent, and when I pull my eyes up to hers, she's white, her mouth gaping.

"Baby, you okay?" I run my fingers along her hairline to tuck a long strand behind her ear.

"He saw Axelle?" She blinks and swings her gaze to mine, color coming back to her cheeks slowly until her expression fires with anger. "He effing confronted *my* daughter!"

I roll my lips between my teeth to avoid laughing.

"He had no right to do that, Blake. And when I was in labor and couldn't protect her." She hammers her fist into the bed. "What a dick!"

"You sayin' no apology then?" A mellow chuckle escapes my lips.

Her eyes meet mine and fury melts into determination. "Tell me you got a good one in, just one solid knock to his jaw."

I shrug one shoulder. "UFL didn't hire me because I make kick-ass cookies, Mouse. What do you think?"

She snorts and nods. "Good."

"Wish I could take credit for the first punch."

Her eyes narrow. "Brae?"

I lift one eyebrow. "Killer."

She sighs and drops her head back to the pillow. "God, I love that kid."

"Pretty sure Killer's after our girl."

"Well, if anyone has the patience for Axelle, it's him."

We sit in silence, Layla staring at Jack, and my eyes bouncing between my son and my woman.

"You tired?"

"Mm-hm." Her head lolls to the side, a peaceful smile on her face. "You want to take him?"

I carefully scoop up my tiny boy and hold him to my chest.

Amazing how quick life can change. There are periods where we soar and some where we plummet, but as long as we hold fast to what matters, fight for the things that count, we die happy knowing we did our best to battle for what matters most.

TWENTY

BLAKE

The sun sinks behind the distant mountains as I rock my son in a chair by the window while Layla sleeps. His face is peaceful as he sleeps except for the occasional baby grunt or twitch of his tiny lips.

His hair is the color of gold and he's got a ton of it. It's hard to say who he resembles more, but I can already tell he's got his mother's nose and her perfect chin. I lean down, placing a kiss on both, overwhelmed with gratitude that a woman as amazing as Layla would fall in love with me. Warts and all.

"You need to eat." Killian has been trying to get Axelle to eat for the past hour, but she refuses. If the tension in his voice is any indication, I'd say he's getting past taking no for an answer. "Come on. Up."

I peek over to see Killer standing, his hand offered to Axelle, but she has her arms crossed at her chest and she's glaring. My lips tick and I turn back to my son to hide my amusement. Stubborn as hell, just like her mother.

"I'm not going, Killian. I'm not leaving my mom."

"I'm taking you to the hospital cafeteria, not fucking Siberia," Killer whisper-hisses and I almost lose my shit and bust up laughing.

She lifts her palm to his face. "Hold on…are you yelling at me in rhymes? This isn't 'Eight Mile,' Eminem."

That's it. I lose it. A long and low chuckle gurgles up my throat and the baby stirs.

"You're a pain in the ass." Killer moves to the door. "I'll grab you something and bring it back." His eyes swing to me. "You want something, man?"

"No thanks, Slim Shady."

Axelle giggles and Killer growls before storming out of the room.

I swivel my chair to face her. "Kiddo…he's right, ya know?"

She crosses her arms over her chest and huffs. "Whatever."

"Why're you so hard on him?"

"I'm not hard on him." She rolls her eyes. "I'm just not hungry."

"Axelle…" There's a warning in my voice that has her up and stomping towards the door.

She glares for a few seconds and pain works behind her eyes. It's as if she knows she's hurting him but can't help it. "Fine. I'll find him." She throws back the door a little harder than she has to.

Poor kid. I feel sorry for Killian. He's had a thing for Axelle from the beginning, but she's been through a lot this last year, and ever since Stew showed up on her doorstep, she hasn't been the same. She'll come around eventually. If Killer wants her bad enough, he'll wait.

My mind spins in one hundred different directions, but I still manage to smile like a damn idiot. Being here in this room with my woman, my ring on her finger, our daughter and newborn son, I feel indestructible. Not at all what I thought I'd feel.

I thought love made me vulnerable. At least, that's the way I was raised. Having no one gives me nothing to lose. Every time I revert to that way of thinking, Layla proves me wrong again and again. Holding my baby in my arms, I feel fear for the future. What kind of hell is this little man going to put me through: fear for his first fever, first broken arm...?

My dad wasn't completely right. Death makes a man think, but so does life.

I hear a soft knock, and Braeden pushes through the door, checks Layla out, and then takes an empty chair and pulls it close. "You gonna let me hold him?"

"No."

"Dude, I sat and had every bone in my hand fractured multiple times with your woman before you got here." He holds his hand up and wiggles his fingers, wincing. "I deserve some uncle-nephew time."

"I gave him your name, dude. That's all you get."

"Seriously?" His eyebrows pinch together. "You're such a baby hog."

I'm half joking with my brother. I don't mind if he holds Jack. I just don't want to let him go. "Fine, but switch spots. He likes being rocked."

Brae takes my place and I lay my son in his arms. "Make sure to support his head."

It takes a few adjustments, but soon Jack is nestled safely in my brother's arms.

I lean in and whisper. "So...Trip?"

"Shit, man." He blows out a long breath. "I'm really sorry about that."

"My woman is stubborn as shit. I knew you didn't have a chance of keeping her out of trouble for twenty-four hours."

"Yeah." He nods. "She's like, some kind of PI ninja with gnarly illusion skills. I seriously believed she was meeting with some mom-to-be-group."

I can't help the rush of pride that swells my chest. "She's a handful, bro."

He turns toward her sleeping. "Yeah…I need to get me one of those."

I smack him upside his head.

"Dude, I'm holding a baby." His whisper-hiss is accompanied by a pretty weak evil-eye.

A chuckle rumbles in my chest, and I swear if I let myself, I'd giggle like a fucking girl. I'm so damn happy.

"How was Dad when you left?" The tiny baby whines and Brae starts rocking.

"Good, man. Really good. I think he's gonna fight."

His eyes grow big with shock. "No kidding?"

I nod and stretch, suddenly feeling tired after today's events. "Yep. He's also planning on coming out for a few days to meet my family."

"Amazing." He goes back to admiring his nephew. "I knew your visiting would be good for him. I think he needed your forgiveness in order to want to go on living."

No kidding? How do I have that much power over a man like Duke Daniels?

I gaze down at my son, who's cradled in my brother's arms, and it hits me. Jack isn't even twenty-four hours old, and already he has me wrapped tightly around his baby finger. If he wanted me to crawl to him on my knees, I'd do it happily. Shit! Talk about a revelation.

"Are you guys talking about your dad?" Layla says, her voice groggy.

"Hey…" I move to her bedside, drop down by her hip, and brush her hair from her face. "How're you feeling?"

Her eyes are a little puffy, but the flush of her cheeks and the undiluted joy that radiates from her smile says it all.

"Better, thanks." She pushes up to sitting. "I'm so sorry I didn't ask about your Dad."

"Nah, don't be." I drop a kiss to her forehead and she closes her eyes and sighs. "It's all good."

"Good? As in…" She doesn't say it, and I don't blame her. It's as if putting the idea in audible words is too much.

"We're good, baby. Facing death has made him see the light."

"Wow, that's great news, Blake." She shifts on the bed, and I prop up some pillows behind her the way the nurses showed me. "Will I finally get to meet them?"

"They're going to make a trip out as soon as you're up for it." A smile pulls at my mouth. God, I must look like a damn clown.

"Knock, knock!" Jonah's voice comes from the door.

"Come in!" Layla pushes herself up, and I pull her blankets up as high as she'll let me and tuck them around her legs.

"You sure? We've got a whole crew in tow." Jonah jerks his head to the people filtering into the room: Raven, Rex, Gia, and Mason whose grimace is apparent. Cameron and Eve trail in behind everyone else, his arm thrown over her shoulder. Ah, there's where Baywatch's mood stems from.

Raven and Eve rush to Layla, and I stand to give them room, but not before lifting Layla's knuckles to my lips for a quick kiss.

Brae doesn't risk standing but swivels his rocker around. "You guys wanna see my amazing little nephew, Jack?"

Rex holds Gia's hand and peers over Brae. "Damn, he looks like you, Layla."

Gia nods. "I love the name. That's the name of a stud."

"Yeah, it is." I grin and cross my arms.

A snort comes from across the room, and Eve has her hand on her chest, silent laughter making her shoulders jump.

"Eve, what the fuck?" Cameron's pinched glare is on his girl.

She stops laughing abruptly as if she'd been poked in the side. "Cameron! You can't cuss around the baby." She shoves him, but he only grabs her arm and pulls her into his chest.

Mason's avoiding them, staring at a bunch of nothing around the room.

"Why you laughin'?" I throw a baby pacifier that Layla has refused to use on Jack, figuring it was expendable. It hits Eve in the back.

"Hey!" She whirls around, but Cam keeps his arms locked around her waist, her back pressed to his front. "It's funny!"

"What's funny?"

"Jack...?" Her eyes move around the room, but everyone is staring at her as if they're waiting for the punch line.

"Axelle Rose...?" Eve rolls her hand through the air, but no one fills in the blank.

"Oh my gosh, people." She slaps her forehead. "Axelle Rose and Jack Daniels! That's so rock n' roll!"

Layla and I find each other's eyes simultaneously, and we're silent for a few beats before we both burst into hysterical laughter.

I sit down on her bed and pull her into my arms. "Our kids are the epitome of rock 'n roll."

She leans into me, laughing. "Let's just hope their names aren't prophetic."

A crowd circles around my baby, and something tells me this is going to be a problem most of his life. With his mom's good looks and my bad attitude, the guy's going to get all kinds of attention, hopefully none of it from the police department.

But even if he did, it wouldn't matter.

Because no matter what he does or what he becomes, I'll never shut him out.

TWENTY-ONE

BLAKE

It's amazing the changes a single day can bring. How holding the fragile life of my son in my arms can bring on an entirely different perspective. It's as if his birth has finally connected me to some kind of parental hard drive. I'm not the same man I was when I rolled out of bed this morning.

I rock back and forth in the dark hospital room while Layla's soft breathing mixes with the tiny snores of our newborn son and lulls me into introspection. Jack in one arm, Layla's phone in my palm, I contemplate what I'm about to do, consider the consequences rather than act on impulse. It's not my usual MO, but it feels right.

Clarity washes over me, and I see things now that I never did before: how a father would go to any length to protect his son, even if that meant sacrificing his relationship with him. I'd never put Jack through what my father put me through, but that doesn't mean I don't finally understand the reasons for why he did what he did.

As frustrating as it is to admit to myself, I can understand why Trip didn't fight for Axelle. According to Layla, he genuinely thought she'd be better off with a guy like Stew, taking the backseat in order for them to have a shot at a decent future. I'm not convinced it's right, but I get it.

I check Layla's phone. It's just past midnight, but something tells me that regardless of the late hour, he'll answer.

I press my lips to my baby's warm cheek. "Come on, bud. We've got business to take care of."

Slowly, I push up from the rocking chair, and with quiet feet, I move out of the room to avoid waking Layla. She was a champion today and has been feeding our son every two hours. The poor woman needs as much sleep as she can get.

Once in the hallway I tiptoe down the quiet corridor to a window that overlooks the city.

"This is the first and most important lesson you'll ever learn in life, Son." Holding up the phone, I scroll through the text messages until I find the one I need. "How to take care of the women you love the most." I hit send and press the phone to my ear.

"Layla?" He answers on the second ring. "Are you okay?"

I grit my teeth at hearing the worry in Trip's voice. "Not Layla, man. It's Blake."

"What do you want?" He's lost the frantic tone and moved straight to asshole. "Another chance to kick my ass?"

I take a deep breath and drop my chin to study my baby's tiny lips as they suckle in his sleep. My son. My blood. What would it have been like to not be here for him? Watch another man raise him as his own?

"Nah, man. Look, I, uh…I'm sorry about what happened earlier." *Kinda.* "I didn't know the whole story, but I wanted you to know that Layla told me everything."

"Oh." He doesn't give me much of an indication as to what he's thinking.

"Here's the thing, Trip. I know you get that my girls went through a lot before moving to Vegas. Things are finally good for them, but that doesn't mean they can shake off seventeen years of bullshit overnight."

"I realize that. I'd just waited so long already. Then hearing what went down with Stew…I needed to find them, make sure they were okay."

"Absolutely. Makes sense you'd do a little snooping, find Layla, and plead your case."

"I didn't mean to hurt them." His voice is low and apologetic.

"I know that. I do." My eyes focus on my Jack's tiny face. "Just took holding my son for me to figure that out."

"A boy, huh? Congratulations."

"Thanks." Yeah, this shit's getting a little too friendly. "I'll make this short. Layla talked about you even before we'd gotten together. You two had a thing that wasn't some little bullshit high school hook up; you made a baby that grew into a young woman whom I love just as much as I do my own blood."

He clears his throat and I know he's feeling this shit. I hate that I'm making him relive it, but he needs to know where we stand so he can respect the boundaries I set moving forward.

"So you fucked up. Now you're straight, but a ton of time has passed, and you dropped a pretty significant bomb when you breezed into town. My girls need a little breathing room while they come to terms with all that."

"Yeah…" He exhales sharply. "You're right. I didn't really think it through. I was too focused on getting to meet my daughter." He seems genuinely apologetic, and, again, I feel as if we're sharing some supersecret dad connection.

"Give them some time. Let them process this shit. When they do, I'll see what I can do about getting Axelle to reach out, yeah?"

"Are you…wait, you're fucking with me, right? I mean you jumped me, and now you're saying you're gonna help me?"

The corner of my mouth twitches at the mix of excitement and confusion in his voice. "If you don't do something to piss me off, yeah, I'll help you."

"I, uh…I appreciate that."

"Don't go thanking me yet. I need you to back off completely for a while. Layla was spitting fire when she found out you approached Axelle without her there. From here on out, no contact: no more digging around, no phone calls, text messages, or emails. Deal?"

"For how long?"

"Until they come around. I'll text you my cell number when we get off the phone. Then I'm going to erase all the history of your calls and texts from Layla's. You have something that needs to be said; you do it through me."

"I don't know. I mean—"

"You want to know your daughter?"

"Of course."

"Then you play by my rules. I won't negotiate on this. You play. I'll do what I can to get her to reach out."

A few beats of silence tick by.

"This is as far as my kindness extends, Trip. We're talking about my family here, my fuckin' reason for breathing. You heard the offer. Take it or leave it."

"Okay, okay. Deal."

"Alright. Now I'm going to let you go, and if you know what's good for you, you'll be on the first flight tomorrow back to your hometown."

"Yeah." He sounds a little pissed, but I don't blame him. He's waited this long to know his daughter, and now he's going to wait longer.

"And, Trip, one last thing."

"What?"

My eyes focus on distant city lights, a world teeming with life. How many lives out there were ever fought for? How many sons and daughters were treated as if they were replaceable?

"I know you have regrets, wish you'd done things differently, but I'm grateful you didn't. Thank you. If it weren't for you, I wouldn't have my girls."

"That's a shitty thing to say, but"—he chuckles—"you're welcome. And thank you for watching out for them."

We hang up and I shoot him a quick text with my number before erasing all his history from the phone. I shove it into my pocket and cradle my son with both arms. "And that's how it's done, bud."

On my way back to Layla's room, it hits me. Trip, The General, and I have a lot more in common than I ever would've thought. We've all made mistakes, screwed up in varying degrees, but we can't allow our mistakes to define our future. We have to look ahead, focus on that next step in the right direction, and fight hard to get what we want, even if that feels like throwing punches to the wind.

At least we fight, and if we go down, we go down swinging.

EPILOGUE

Six months later...

LAYLA

"For the love of God, Layla, can we please do this already?" Braeden groans and drops his head back. He's standing with his thumbs hooked into his pockets, leaning against the wall, looking every bit the military hero in his dress blues.

"Okay, I'm ready." I take a deep breath and check my reflection one last time.

"You've been doing that for ten minutes." He pushes off the wall, glaring at me through the mirror. "Pretty sure a guy ain't going to show up in your reflection to tell you you're the fairest of them all anytime soon."

I whirl around and glare at him. "Hardy har har."

He takes me in from my hair to my feet, and his eyes soften when they land on my shoes. "A wedding dress and biker boots." He shakes his head. "You were so made for my brother." He holds out his arm and nods for me to take it.

"Thank you." I slip my hand into the crook of his elbow. "I'll take that as a compliment."

"As you should." He flashes that Daniels' crooked grin. "You're the most beautiful bride I've ever seen." A hint of color touches his cheeks. "Definitely the fairest in the land."

"Aww…" Hot tears burn my eyes. "No, no, no!" I stomp my foot. "You're going to make me cry, and it took Eve thirty minutes to get these fake eyelashes on straight." I pretend I'm checking my eyelashes and not actually soaking up the beginning stages of tears.

He chuckles as we move from the bride's room into the reception area of the church. It wasn't our idea to get married in a house of God, but Blake wanted a traditional wedding to honor our parents' beliefs and customs.

At first I thought it was absurd. I mean we already live together and have a baby, but I love how committed Blake is to ensuring our parents are proud and comfortable with our situation.

That's also the reason I'm wearing a white dress. The Lord God above knows I sure don't deserve it, but Blake insisted I deserve to wear white more than any other bride because I never had the option to do it the other way.

"Your choices were taken away from you, Mouse. I want you to have them back. You want to wear white; you fucking do it and own it. Throw a big fat middle finger to the past, and take control of your future."

I went shopping with Axelle, Raven, Eve, and Gia the weekend after Jack was born and fell in love with a corset-style wedding dress with a black lace overlay on the bodice. Everything about it screamed rock n' roll, and without even checking the price tag, I agreed to buy it.

Standing outside the double doors that enter into the chapel, I fuss with my hair. Blake loves it down, so I had Eve style it in long, loose curls that hang around my shoulders, and instead of a veil, I opted for a thick black fabric that wears like a headband and ties at the nape of my neck.

The church wedding coordinator presses her eye between the doors that lead into the sanctuary. "It's almost time, you two, ready?"

Brae looks down at me, grinning. "You ready—"

"Wait!" I hold my finger up to the lady and turn to face Brae head on. "I forgot to say thank you for doing this. My dad…his wheel chair…I just…"

"I'm honored." He squeezes my hand and tucks it back into the bend of his arm. "Now let's do this. Last time I was left in charge of you I fucked it up, and my brother swore wedgies and loogie drops to my forehead if I fucked it up again."

"Well, we can't have that." With my blood-red rose bouquet held to my waist, I squeeze my future brother-in-law's arm. "I'm ready."

BLAKE

Standing up here in front of all these people, wearing a damn monkey suit couldn't feel any more awkward. Over two hundred of our friends and family sit facing me while I wait for Brae to walk Layla down the aisle.

I keep my shoulders back, arms loose, hands clasped in front of me. The small string quartet plays a familiar wedding song, but as I stand here getting ready to make my woman my wife, the melody sounds new, as if it were created just for us.

My eyes scan the room, passing over all the gazes set on me, to settle on my dad. Over the last six months, he's endured rigorous amounts of chemotherapy and radiation. His once strong body is now almost half its size, his skin pale and almost hanging off his bones in some places just like the starched fabric of his dress blues. The small bit of hair that's finally growing back on his chemo-ravaged scalp is completely white.

But his eyes shine with a ferocity I've never seen in him before. His posture is that of man ten times his size and weight, and he gazes up at me with the pride of a father who has spent his entire life hero-worshipping a son. Our eyes lock. He nods and it's so small, but it communicates support and love.

My mom has her hands wrapped around one of his in her lap, and she smiles in a way that seems to say, *I knew you'd be okay.*

Layla's mom and dad are sitting together in the front row on the opposite side from my parents. They were older when they had Layla and now look more like great-grandparents. We were able to fly them in town and arranged for a nurse to accompany them. When I called Layla's dad back before I proposed, I told him I'd make sure he was there to give his daughter away. He didn't believe I could make it happen, but now he gets it. I'd do anything, pay any amount, cross to the ends of the world and beyond if it meant making my woman happy.

A baby-sized squeal comes from behind me, and I turn to see Axelle moving to her spot across from me with Jack in her arms.

"Sorry," she mouths and moves into her position as Maid of Honor. "Diaper change."

Jack squeals and flashes a toothless grin before leaning forward to gum his sister's shoulder. I roll my lips between my teeth to avoid laughing, at the same time thinking we need to move this along because Jack clearly needs to feed.

The sound of the quartet fades, and then they start up a new song that has the entire room standing and turning toward the back of the sanctuary. My stomach flip flops with excitement, and I stand tall, my eyes fixed to the back of the room.

The double doors swing open, and with the mid-day sun shining behind her, I can only make out her silhouette. That alone has my knees wobbling and me holding my breath.

An angel.

She's my fucking angel.

One slow step at a time, Braeden walks Layla toward me until she's fully visible beneath the lights. Her big brown eyes set on mine and I catch my breath. My hand moves to my chest of its own accord as if trying to protect my heart from her beauty.

They continue to advance, not fucking fast enough, as the music plays.

Gorgeous.

Breathtaking.

One of a kind.

The whispers of the people in the audience mimic my thoughts.

As they reach the end of the aisle, Layla's eyes break from mine to watch as Braeden wheels her father to her right side. He's hunched over in his chair, unable to sit up fully, so Layla squats at his side, pulling one of his shaky hands into hers, then turns to face the pastor.

"Who gives this woman to be married to this man?" the pastor says with a Bible clutched to his chest.

Layla's dad sits up as tall as he can, throwing back his shoulders just as I've seen her do countless times. "Her mother and I do." He places a tender kiss to her knuckles then holds out her hand to me.

My heart leaps in my chest. I already have Layla in every way a man possibly can, but something about the act of having her handed off to me by the man who gave her life and nurtured her to be the woman she is, pulls something deep within me. Humility and feelings of unworthiness wash over me, and I claim Layla's hand and bend to meet her father's eyes.

"Mr. Devereux, thank you for trusting me to take care of your daughter. I won't let you down, sir."

His bottom lip quivers, foggy brown eyes shine with tears, but he remains stoic. "No, I don't believe you will."

Layla and I stand, and Brae wheels her father back before taking his place at my side. We turn hand in hand to the pastor, and I can't help peeking over at her. Her face is made up just enough to enhance her already perfect features, lips painted a deep red that reminds me of a ripe cherry. She sees me staring and smiles so sweetly that my heart kicks double-time. I'm surprised I turn back to the pastor without pulling her in for a long, deep, wet kiss.

Patience, Daniels. That part's coming.

"Ladies and Gentlemen, we are gathered here today..."

The ceremony goes on exactly how we rehearsed. There are tears, laughter, more tears, and the occasional baby protest. I try as hard as I can to keep my head in the game, remember all my lines when the time comes, but it's difficult to focus on anything except Layla.

She radiates purity and love in white, but the black lace that pushes up her breasts and those damn biker boots scream rebel. My hands itch to explore her body, to see all that fabric pooled around her ankles as I run my tongue over every inch of her naked skin.

"You may kiss the bride."

"Fuckin' finally," I murmur and receive a tight warning glare from the pastor.

"I cannot believe you just said the f-word in church," Layla whispers, but the ginormous grin on her face contradicts her reprimand.

I cup her face in my hands, lean down, and brush my lips against hers. "Open up, Mrs. Daniels. Let's give them a show they'll never forget."

—

Six hours later...

LAYLA

We burst through the doors of our honeymoon suite, with me cradled in Blake's arms and our mouths fused together. I don't know how he managed to work the key card without looking, but I'm damn grateful he did.

Blake rips his mouth from mine. "Shit, Mouse. Are you trying to get us blacklisted from The Four Seasons?"

I push up, pressing my breasts to his chest and pulling his lips back to mine. "I could ask you the same thing." Our voices are breathless and weak.

What started out as innocent kissing in the elevator quickly turned to fondling, which will ignite into a full-blown public indecency charge if we don't get our asses behind closed doors ASAP.

The reception was beautiful. Food was delicious. Decorations flawless. But I still found myself wanting to hit fast forward on the night and get to our suite. I longed for it to be just the two of us, alone for the first time as husband and wife.

Blake drops my legs so my feet hit the floor but doesn't release me from the beautiful assault of his tongue.

I moan and pull back to meet his eyes, which are hooded and practically glowing emerald. "Are you going to rob me of my first look around this fancy hotel room?"

He shrugs off his tux jacket without leaving my space. His eyes roam my neck, jawline, and breasts. "'Fraid so. You'll have to take in the sights when you're on all fours." He steps close, wound up tight after today, and I step back out of instinct. "Study the ceiling when you're on your back." Having already removed his tie earlier, he moves to unbutton his black dress shirt. "Check out the view while I'm taking you on your side."

My stomach tumbles and melts down low. I step back again, only to have him chase me down. His hands move to the swell of my breasts, which are now heaving and practically spilling over my corset top. He traces the line of my cleavage. "Want this off, but the way I'm feeling, I don't want to rip it."

A giggle burns in my chest but dies before it hits my lips. I turn around and pull my hair over one shoulder while he slowly unlaces the delicate fabric and pushes it down around my hips and then to the floor. The cool air hits my body and I shiver. He must've chucked his shirt, because I feel his bare skin against my back and his hands slide around my belly.

I've lost most of the baby weight I'd gained during pregnancy, but my tummy isn't as flat or tight as it used to be. Now to accompany the C-section scar I got bringing Axelle into the world, I've got a few extra stretch marks too, but I'd never know it from the way Blake feasts his eyes on me.

If anything, he seems more attracted to me now that I've got the battle wounds of childbirth marking my body. He treats them like medals, symbols of valor that he insists on worshiping with his hands and lips whenever we make love.

"No bra?" He cups my swollen breasts, still larger from breastfeeding.

I tilt my head and allow him better access to my throat and jaw. "The top of my dress held everything in place, and I had to pump a couple times. No bra equals easy access."

The vibration of his laughter rolls across my skin in a sensual caress. "Easy access is my favorite, Mouse."

His mouth continues its torturous exploration while his hands drop lower and trace the line of my lace panties. I moan as his fingers slip below the delicate fabric and move straight between my legs. I bite my lip and roll against his hand, hoping he picks up on my unspoken request.

He nuzzles my neck, nips my ear, and then freezes. "You sure we left Axelle and my parents with enough milk?"

I blink open my eyes and feel cool air hit my upper back as he leans to meet my glare.

"The pediatrician said he'd have a growth spurt at six months. I'd hate it if he burned through all you pumped and didn't have—"

"Blake"—I drop my chin to my chest—"we've been over this."

"Yeah, I know, but—"

I turn around, losing his hand that was between my legs, not that it matters since this conversation has doused my arousal. He opens his mouth, but I put my finger to his lips.

"No." I shake my head. "It's our wedding night. I've had to look at you all night and imagine all the dirty things you'd do to me once we were finally in our room, and I refuse to allow you to ruin it by worrying." He kisses my finger, and I drop it from his lips with no intention of allowing him to continue before I set the ground rules. "First, no mention of any of our parents. Let's face it. They're the last people we should be thinking about when we're naked. Our kids are a close second, but we can't not talk about them, so let's save them for post-lovemaking conversation. And third, for the hundredth time, Jack has plenty of milk, and they're staying in the same hotel, so if worse comes to worse, Axelle can bring him to us." I hold out my hand and make a show of dropping the mic.

He tilts his head, one eye squinting. "You've been imagining all the dirty things I'd do to you?"

"Seriously? That's all you heard?" I huff out a breath, blowing a strand of my long hair off my face. "Yes, I have. I figured you had big wedding night sex plans. I'd hoped they'd have nothing to do with discussions about pumping milk."

He sifts his thick fingers through my hair and cups my head. "Oh I do, baby." He doesn't close his eyes as he drops small kisses all over my face. "And they start with"—more kisses—"a long bath in that Jacuzzi."

I suck in a breath and lean to see behind him and into the bathroom. "We have a Jacuzzi?"

He scoops me up, and I squeak in surprise as he moves us into a bathroom that's as large as our living room with marble everything, a his and her shower with glass walls, and—holy crap—a tub for four that buts up to a huge glass window overlooking the Las Vegas Strip.

He places me down at the edge of the tub and moves to plug it and run the water. I can't help but eat up the visual of his body as he leans his bare torso around to twist and turn nobs, searching for the perfect combination of hot and cold. His muscles roll beneath his smooth skin, and his side tattoos draw my eyes, reminding me of the first time we made love: the first time Blake showed me that he owned my body as much as he owned my heart, even if I wasn't aware of it yet.

He stands me up and drags my panties down so I can step out of them. He holds my hand, and I step into the warm water before dropping down and sinking in up to my neck.

"You look good enough to eat in there, Mouse." His eyes cast a glow of pure sexual heat as he watches me while unbuttoning his dress pants and then pushing them along with his boxer briefs to the floor.

My eyes widen as he moves toward me to crawl into the tub. No matter how many times I see Blake, I'll never get tired of his body. Strong, powerful, and capable. A tremor of need races down my spine as he stays standing, towering over me, his feet between my legs and just under my knees.

"Fuck, I love it when you look at me like that. I can feel your eyes on me and love watching you plan your next move."

He knows me so well. I blush, thankful that the warm water already has my face flushed. My hand moves to his hard-on without me telling it to, and I stroke him with wet hands. His hips jerk into my touch, and I bring my second hand up to join the first.

Mesmerized, I watch as he tightens and swells with every long, firm glide of my hands. His legs slightly open, he rocks into my grip but sucks in a breath and pulls my hands off him.

I gasp at the sudden move. "What's wrong?"

He sits down in the tub, facing me, then grabs my hips and pulls me up to straddle his lap. I cry out in pleasure as his hard length lies between my legs.

"Not a damn thing is wrong. Just want my wedding night to last longer than five minutes. I need to set the bar high for a lifetime of good sex, baby. That's a tall order." His arms move around and squeeze my ass while pushing me down and up, sliding himself against me.

I brace my hands behind my back to leverage my weight, and he continues to jack himself off against my body. His powerful arms flex as he works us both into a frenzy, and an intense longing stirs my gut.

"Blake, I need you. Please…" My words dissolve on a moan as he finds the spot that makes me crazy.

"I'm right here with you, Mouse." His breathless growl only pushes me farther, and I feel the tingling of my building release as it powers between my legs.

Our breathless moans and the gentle slapping of the water fill the room. I push up, plant my hands on his chest, and cover his mouth with mine. Our tongues tangle together in a flurry of lips and pulls of our teeth. I arch my back so that every push-pull of our bodies drags my nipples along his chest.

"I'm gonna come, baby. Just like this. Not even inside you yet, and I'm done."

I sneak my hand around my back. On the up pass, I guide him to me and sink down.

"Fuuuck…" he groans at being buried on surprise.

Unable to stop reaching for the release that is so close it feels like a tease, I ride him hard and fast. He leans back in the bath, hands to my hips, matching each drop with a thrust of his own.

I flatten my hands against his pecs and lock eyes with him as our bodies take over and bring us both to the brink. My stomach tightens, thighs quiver, and right then his hands move up to knead my breasts. "My wife."

The mixture of possession and tender awe in his voice sends me over the edge. Light explodes behind my eyes, and I grind down on his body. My forehead falls to his shoulder, and I hold onto him with my teeth as the orgasm rolls through me in wave after wave of euphoria. I'm lightheaded and panting as I resurface. "My husband."

The last syllable is barely out when he moves and flips me to all fours so that I'm facing out to the brilliant Vegas skyline. Before I can even enjoy the view, he grips my hips and slams into me from behind. I gasp at the delicious stretch of this position and lean back, hoping to get more of him.

"So fucking perfect." He moves, not slowly, but on a mission. "My woman." He thrusts and grinds, coaxing me into another orgasm. "My Mouse." His slick hands glide up my spine and move around to cup my breasts. "My wife."

His teeth clamp down on my shoulder, and he groans long and heavy into my neck. I whimper at the pleasure-pain of his bite combined with the heat of his release. We're both breathing hard, his chest to my back, as we come back to ourselves.

My arms shake with the effort it takes to hold myself up and above the water, but before I can squirm away, he pushes back to lie in the bath and takes me with him. He positions me between his legs, and we stare out at the city.

"What do you think of married life so far?" I flick the glassy surface of the warm water, a huge ass smile on my face.

"It's exactly what I thought it'd be. Wish I could've convinced you to do it sooner."

I shrug and run my hands up and down his powerful thighs. "The best things come to those who wait."

"I believe that." His voice has taken on a serious tone. He grabs my chin to tilt my face to the side forcing my eyes to his. "I'd have waited forever. Swear to God if I'd known back then that everything I had to go through would one day bring me here, to our wedding night, naked and wrapped around you like this, I'd gladly do it all again. I'd walk through hell and back if it meant the rest of my life with you."

A single tear races down my cheek, but before it hits the water, he hooks it with his finger and sucks it into his mouth. "Happy tears."

"Yeah." My one word answer hitches on a soft whimper.

"And from here on out that's all I'll ever give you, baby." He snags another tear with a fingertip.

"I can't believe I finally found you." After Stewart and Trip, I realized that I'd never felt real love for a man before. I wouldn't have known it even existed if I hadn't seen in in the eyes of other couples. But then I met Blake and I knew. This kind of love isn't a fairy tale meant for dreamers or stuck in the pages of books. It's real, all-consuming, and soul deep, and now, here, lying in the arms of my husband, I've never felt more convinced. "You're my true love. My first and only true love, Blake."

"And you're mine." He brings my hand to his lips and slides soft kisses against my skin. "First...and last."

~The End~

ACKNOWLEDGMENTS

First I want to thank God who gave me the imagination to create stories and the ability to tell them.

Thank you to my husband and my children who inspire my characters more than I'll ever admit to.

I want to thank all the girls (and boy) in The Fighting Girls Fun Cage on Facebook. Not a day goes by where I don't pop in there and leave feeling so full of love and hope. I don't know what I'd do without you.

Evelyn Johnson, your support and friendship have been my anchor. This adventure has been so much fun with you at my side. Here's to more in 2015!

Amanda "PIMA" Simpson, thank you for being my sounding board, my graphic artist, but most importantly my friend. I don't know where I would be without you, and not a day goes by that I'm not overwhelmed with gratitude for everything you've taught me and continue to do for my business.

Thank you to Theresa Wegand Proofreading & Editing for sticking with me through five books now. I'm looking forward to your perfecting many more of my books in the future. It's so much fun working with you.

My books would be crap if it weren't for the expertise of The Sexy Six Critter Crew: Cristin "Spice" Harber, Claudia "Dia" Handel, Sharon "Shex" Cermak, Racquel "Rox" Reck, and Nicola "Nic" Layouni. If this writing thing ended tomorrow, we'd make one kickass crew of commando ninja PI warriors. Love you girls.

To Elizabeth Reyes for being a guiding force, thank you. I can't believe here I am, five books later, and none of it would've happened if it weren't for your encouragement.

Thank you to the amazing authors who inspire me every day with their writing, positive attitudes, and their appreciation for their readers.

Thank you to everyone who has given The Fighting Series a chance. I'll never be able to express adequately how much your faith in my writing means to me.

ABOUT THE AUTHOR

JB Salsbury, New York Times Best Selling author of the Fighting series, lives in Phoenix, Arizona, with her husband and two kids. She spends the majority of her day as a domestic engineer. But while she works through her daily chores, a world of battling alphas, budding romance, and impossible obstacles claws away at her subconscious, begging to be released to the page.

Her love of good storytelling led her to earn a degree in Media Communications. With her journalistic background, writing has always been at the forefront, and her love of romance prompted her to sink her free time into novel writing.

For more information on the series or just to say hello, visit JB on her website, Facebook, or Goodreads page.

http://www.jbsalsbury.com/
https://www.facebook.com/JBSalsburybooks
http://www.goodreads.com/author/
show/6888697.Jamie_Salsbury

Made in the USA
San Bernardino, CA
01 October 2015